HERОD

The Architect of Power

D. DECKKER

Dinsu Books

This novel is a work of historical fiction. While inspired by historical events and figures, including Herod the Great and the Second Temple in Jerusalem, the story incorporates fictionalized elements, characters, and events for dramatic and narrative purposes. Certain details have been imagined or reinterpreted to enhance the storytelling experience. The book does not claim to be a definitive historical account and should not be used as a primary source for historical research. Readers are encouraged to explore additional scholarly resources for a more comprehensive understanding of the historical context.

ISBN-13: 9798304401715

Cover design by: D. DECKKER
Printed in the United States of America

To Subhashini, my beloved wife, whose unwavering support and brilliance inspire me every day.

And to Sasha, our wonderful daughter, who fills my life with joy and wonder.

This book is for you, with all my love.

CONTENTS

INTRODUCTION

The year is 37 BCE. The sands of Judea shift under the weight of Roman boots, and the air hums with the tension of a kingdom on the brink. Herod, the son of Antipater, stands at a crossroads, his path forged by ambition and fear, his destiny intertwined with the will of Rome. At the age of twenty-five, he is already a man of contrasts—a warrior with the intellect of a statesman, a ruler with the heart of a survivor.

To understand Herod is to understand the forces that shaped him: the ruthless pragmatism of his father, Antipater, who taught him that fear is the foundation of power; the volatile politics of a region caught between independence and imperial domination; and the personal betrayals that etched distrust deep into his soul. Judea, a land of prophets and kings, now kneels before the might of Rome, and Herod must navigate a labyrinth of alliances and rivalries to secure his place in history.

But Herod's story is not merely one of conquest and governance. It is a story of ambition turned obsession, love turned tragedy, and legacy turned enigma. As he ascends to power, the young king grapples with the weight of expectation, the shadows of betrayal, and the haunting realization that greatness often demands sacrifice—of others, and of oneself.

This tale begins not with a crown, but with a choice. A choice to rise above the chaos or be consumed by it. To wield power or be crushed by its burden. To build a legacy that will endure the ages, even as it exacts a devastating toll.

Herod's life is a reminder that history is not written in black and white, but in shades of ambition, loyalty, and betrayal. And as you turn the pages of this story, you will find not just a king, but a man —flawed, complex, and unforgettable.

PREFACE

History often remembers Herod the Great as a paradoxical figure—a visionary architect who left behind some of the ancient world's most awe-inspiring marvels, and a ruthless ruler whose paranoia and ambition knew no bounds. He is a man shrouded in both grandeur and infamy, a symbol of the complex interplay between power and legacy.

This novel seeks to delve into the life of Herod, exploring not just the towering achievements for which he is celebrated, but also the human cost of his relentless ambition. What drives a man to build monuments that defy time while tearing apart the lives of those closest to him? How does a ruler navigate the thin line between strength and tyranny, loyalty and betrayal, love and fear?

Through a narrative that blends historical accuracy with creative interpretation, *Herod: The Architect of Power* aims to bring to life the world of ancient Judea, the tensions of Roman politics, and the personal struggles of a king torn between his desires and his demons. While inspired by recorded history, this story also ventures into the uncharted spaces of Herod's inner world, imagining the thoughts, motivations, and conflicts that may have shaped his decisions.

It is important to note that this book is not a scholarly account but a work of historical fiction. Certain events, characters, and dialogues have been fictionalized to deepen the emotional and psychological exploration of Herod's life. Readers seeking historical accuracy should complement this novel with academic resources.

As you journey through the pages of this story, you will encounter a man who is as much a product of his time as he is a force of nature. Herod's legacy is one of contradictions: a builder and a destroyer, a ruler and a tyrant, a man who sought eternity but was consumed by the fragility of his power.

May this tale illuminate the shadows of history and offer a glimpse into the soul of a man who, even in death, refuses to be forgotten.

CHAPTER 1: THE KINGMAKER'S SON

The desert sun cast long, jagged shadows across the limestone walls of Antipater's estate, where the scent of olive oil and dust mingled in the still air. The young Herod stood at the edge of the courtyard, watching his father, Antipater, orchestrate a meeting of Judean elders. The men's voices were low and conspiratorial, their words a careful balance of respect and ambition. Even at twelve years old, Herod could sense the weight of the moment, though he could not yet name the power that drove his father to maneuver these men as if they were pieces on a chessboard.

Antipater was a man of calculation, his every gesture deliberate, every word wielded like a blade. He turned toward Herod and caught his son staring. For a brief moment, a flicker of pride crossed his weathered face, but it disappeared as quickly as it had come.

"Herod, come here," Antipater commanded, his tone carrying the authority of a man who had won Rome's favor and lived to wield it.

Herod hesitated, his bare feet skimming the sunbaked stones of the courtyard. He stepped forward, each movement made a deliberate effort to appear composed, though his heart beat furiously in his chest.

“These men will shape the future of Judea,” Antipater said, gesturing to the elders. “If you are to succeed me, you must learn to shape them in turn.”

The boy’s gaze flickered to the men, their faces a tapestry of creased brows and thin-lipped determination. They looked at him with measured curiosity, as if weighing his potential. He felt small under their scrutiny, but he straightened his shoulders and met their eyes.

Antipater turned back to the elders. “We face threats from within and without,” he said, his voice smooth and commanding. “Rome demands stability, and Judea cannot afford weakness. Our strength lies in unity, and unity requires decisive leadership.”

One of the elders, his beard streaked with gray, nodded slowly. “You speak wisely, Antipater. But wisdom alone will not quell dissent. What do you propose?”

Antipater’s smile was razor-sharp. “A demonstration of loyalty. Let the people see that we are united in purpose, that any who challenge us will face the consequences.”

The elder’s eyes narrowed. “And if Rome questions our methods?”

Antipater leaned forward, his voice dropping to a conspiratorial whisper. “Rome respects strength. They will not question what they cannot afford to acknowledge.”

Herod watched, mesmerized, as his father’s words wove a web of authority and compliance. It was not just the content of Antipater’s speech but the way he delivered; each phrase calculated to appeal to ambition, fear, and the desire for survival.

That evening, Antipater called Herod to his study. The room was dimly lit, the scent of parchment and ink filling the air. Antipater sat behind a massive wooden desk, a map of Judea spread before him.

“A king requires fear,” Antipater began, his voice steady. “Without it, wisdom is ignored, strength is challenged, and loyalty is betrayed." He gestured to the map, his fingers tracing the borders of Judea. "This land is a crucible. It will test you, bend you, and if you are not careful, it will break you. Do you understand?"

Herod nodded, though he felt the weight of the lesson pressing down on him. "Yes, Father."

Antipater's gaze bore into him. "Words are easy, boy. Power is not. You must wield it with precision. Take Marcus Septimus, for example. Do you think he respects me because I flatter him? No. He respects me because he fears what I can do if he does not."

Herod's brows furrowed. "But if they fear you, won't they also hate you?"

Antipater's lips curled into a cold smile. "Let them hate, so long as they obey. A king cannot afford love. **Love makes you weak. Remember that.**"

The lessons continued that evening as Antipater hosted a feast for visiting Roman officials. The villa was a cacophony of laughter, clinking goblets, and the scent of roasted lamb. Herod watched from a corner as his father moved through the crowd with the precision of a lion stalking prey. Antipater's every gesture exuded confidence, his words calculated to charm and disarm the Romans while subtly reminding them of his indispensability.

Herod's eyes lingered on one man in particular: Marcus Septimus, a Roman envoy with a stern jaw and a voice that seemed to fill the room. Herod had overheard his father's advisors discussing the man's importance in securing Judea's future. Antipater's interactions with Marcus were a delicate dance, each move designed to extract favor without overstepping.

"Do you see that man?" Antipater's voice cut through Herod's thoughts. His father had appeared beside him, his expression unreadable.

Herod nodded. "Marcus Septimus."

"Good. Watch him closely. Men like him can make or unmake kings." Antipater's gaze darkened. "But never trust them. The

Romans will feed you with one hand while sharpening a dagger in the other."

Herod swallowed hard, the image of a dagger embedding itself in his mind.

Later that night, Herod sat in the quiet solitude of the courtyard, the stars overhead shimmering like scattered coins. His mind was a whirl of his father's words, the weight of expectations pressing down on him. He felt a strange mix of pride and fear, the realization that his path was one of both greatness and peril.

"You think too much for a boy your age," a voice called out. Herod turned to see Matthias, his childhood friend, approaching. Matthias carried the carefree air of someone unburdened by destiny, his face lit with an easy grin.

"And you don't think enough," Herod replied, though his tone lacked malice. Matthias laughed and plopped down beside him, the warmth of his presence a small comfort.

"Your father is a great man," Matthias said. "Everyone says so. They say you will be even greater."

Herod looked at his friend, the words both a balm and a burden. "Do you think I will?"

Matthias shrugged. "I think you will do whatever you must."

The answer unsettled Herod. There was something too knowing in Matthias's tone, as if he had glimpsed a part of Herod that even Herod himself did not fully understand.

A week later, Herod's world shifted.

Antipater had summoned his advisors to discuss a matter of great importance. Herod, eager to prove himself, insisted on attending. The meeting took place in a chamber filled with the heavy aroma of incense and tension.

As the men spoke of alliances and threats, Herod noticed Matthias lingering at the edge of the room, his expression uneasy. The boy's presence was unusual, and Herod felt a prickle of unease.

"What brings you here, Matthias?" Herod asked, his tone light but probing.

Matthias hesitated, his gaze darting to Antipater. "I came to deliver a message," he said finally, his voice strained.

Before Herod could press further, the doors burst open, and a group of Roman soldiers entered, their presence a sudden storm in the quiet chamber. The leader, Marcus Septimus, strode forward, his expression grim.

"Antipater," he said, his voice cold. "You have been accused of conspiring against Rome."

The room erupted into chaos. Herod's heart pounded as he turned to Matthias, the truth dawning on him in a sickening wave. His friend—his trusted companion—had betrayed them.

"Matthias, what have you done?" Herod's voice cracked with disbelief.

Matthias avoided his gaze, shame and fear warring on his face. "I didn't have a choice," he whispered. "They would have killed my family."

Herod's world tilted. The betrayal cut deeper than any dagger, carving a wound that would never fully heal. He watched as Antipater was led away, the weight of his father's warning echoing in his mind: Never forget that power is a fragile thing.

In the days that followed, Herod's grief and rage festered like an open wound. He confronted Matthias in the same courtyard where they had once shared laughter under the stars.

"You were my friend," Herod said, his voice trembling with fury. "I trusted you."

Matthias fell to his knees, tears streaming down his face. "I had no choice, Herod. They would have killed everyone I loved."

Herod stared at him, his emotions a storm of anger, betrayal, and something darker—a cold, calculating resolve. He stepped forward, his shadow falling over Matthias like a shroud.

“I will never forget this,” Herod said, his voice low and icy. “And neither will you.”

He turned and walked away, leaving Matthias sobbing in the dust. It was the first time Herod truly understood the cost of trust, and the lesson would stay with him for the rest of his life.

CHAPTER 2: GOVERNOR OF GALILEE

The rugged hills of Galilee stretched endlessly under the pale morning light, their jagged peaks clawing at the sky. Herod rode at the front of his company, his cloak billowing in the wind, the scent of damp earth and olive groves filling his nostrils. Behind him, a contingent of soldiers followed in grim silence, their armor glinting as the sun broke through the haze. It was a land as wild and untamed as the men who plagued it—bandits who had turned the region into a crucible of fear.

Herod had been appointed governor by his father's decree, a decision endorsed by the Romans. His mission was clear: bring order to the chaos and make Galilee an example of Roman-aligned governance. The weight of expectation sat heavily on his shoulders, but beneath it burned a resolve that had been forged in the fires of betrayal. This was his chance to prove his worth, not only to his father but to the Romans who held the true power.

As they approached a village rumored to harbor bandits, Herod raised his hand, signaling the soldiers to halt. The village lay in a shallow valley, its stone houses huddled together like frightened sheep. Smoke curled lazily from a handful of chimneys, and the faint sound of laughter carried on the wind. It was deceptively peaceful.

"Surround it," Herod ordered, his voice calm but laced with authority. The soldiers obeyed without hesitation, fanning out to encircle the settlement. Herod dismounted, his boots crunching against the gravel as he strode toward the village center.

The headman emerged, a wiry figure with a face carved by years of hardship. He approached Herod cautiously, his hands raised in a gesture of submission.

"My lord," the man began, his voice trembling. "We are simple folk. Farmers and shepherds. We have nothing to hide."

Herod studied the man, his dark eyes unblinking. He had learned to read people, to sense the truth beneath their words. "Bandits have been attacking travelers along this route," he said. "They take refuge in the hills, but they are fed and sheltered by villages like this one. Tell me where they are, and I will spare your people."

The headman's expression faltered, a flicker of fear crossing his face. "I swear, my lord, we know nothing of these men."

Herod stepped closer, his voice dropping to a whisper. "Lies have a way of unraveling, old man. If I discover you are protecting them, your village will burn, and your people will pay the price."

The headman's shoulders sagged under the weight of Herod's gaze. "There is a cave," he confessed finally, his voice barely audible. "To the north, in the hills. They use it as their base."

Herod nodded, his expression inscrutable. "You've chosen wisely." He turned to his captain. "Gather the men. We move at once."

The cave was a jagged wound on the hillside, hidden among a cluster of gnarled trees. Herod and his soldiers approached with caution; the air heavy with anticipation. He could feel the tension crackling around him, the quiet before the storm.

"No survivors," Herod said coldly, his voice cutting through the silence. The soldiers nodded grimly; their weapons drawn.

The attack was swift and merciless. Herod led the charge, his sword flashing as he cut down the first bandit who emerged from the cave. The air was filled with the clash of steel and the guttural cries of men fighting for their lives. Blood spattered the rocky ground, mingling with the dust.

Herod fought with a ferocity that surprised even himself, each strike of his blade a release of the anger and betrayal that had simmered within him since Matthias's treachery. By the time the battle ended, the cave was silent, its shadows hiding the broken bodies of the bandits.

Herod stood at the entrance, his chest heaving, his sword dripping with blood. Around him, the soldiers gathered, their expressions a mix of triumph and horror. He felt no remorse, only a grim satisfaction. Order had been restored, and his authority cemented.

Word of Herod's ruthlessness spread quickly. The bandits who had terrorized Galilee for years began to vanish, their ranks thinning as fear took root. Herod's name became a whispered warning, a symbol of swift and unrelenting justice.

But with power came new challenges. The Hasmoneans, a once-powerful dynasty now diminished, watched Herod's rise with wary eyes. Among them was Alexandra, matriarch of the family, and her daughter, Mariamne. They represented a political alliance Herod's father had carefully cultivated, but it was an alliance fraught with tension.

Mariamne was introduced to Herod during a feast at the governor's residence. The room was alight with the glow of oil lamps, their golden light reflecting off polished stone walls. The scent of roasted meat and spices filled the air, mingling with the low hum of conversation.

Herod noticed her immediately. She was striking, her beauty softened by an air of quiet strength. Her dark eyes met his, unflinching, and for a moment, the noise of the room faded into silence.

“Governor Herod,” Alexandra said, her tone polite but guarded. “This is my daughter, Mariamne.”

Herod inclined his head, his gaze never leaving Mariamne’s. “It is an honor,” he said, his voice smooth. “Your reputation precedes you.”

Mariamne’s lips curved into a faint smile. “I hope it does so favorably.”

Herod chuckled, a rare warmth in his voice. “More than favorably. The Hasmonean legacy is one of great strength and wisdom. Judea owes much to your family.”

Alexandra watched the exchange carefully, her expression unreadable. She was a woman who understood the art of politics, and she saw in Herod a man who could be both ally and adversary.

After the feast, Herod found himself thinking of Mariamne. There was something about her that intrigued him, quiet confidence that set her apart. He saw in her the possibility of a union that could solidify his position and bridge the divide between his Idumean roots and the Hasmonean dynasty.

But he also saw the danger. The Hasmoneans were not to be underestimated, and Alexandra’s ambitions were as sharp as any blade. Herod knew that any alliance with them would come at a cost.

In the weeks that followed, Herod worked tirelessly to strengthen his hold on Galilee. He imposed strict laws, rebuilt crumbling infrastructure, and ensured the Romans saw him as an effective governor. But the specter of the Hasmoneans loomed, a reminder that his position was far from secure.

One evening, as Herod walked the walls of the city he now governed, he allowed himself a moment of reflection. The stars above were bright and cold, their light casting long shadows on the stones beneath his feet. He thought of Matthias, of the betrayal that had shaped him, and of the path that lay ahead. He had proven his ruthlessness, but he knew it was only the beginning. To truly secure his place, he would need to navigate the treacherous waters of politics with the same precision he had wielded his sword in the hills of Galilee.

As the wind whispered through the olive trees, Herod made a silent vow. He would rise above the chaos, above the whispers of doubt and fear. He would build a legacy that would outlast the stars themselves. And he would let nothing—and no one—stand in his way.

CHAPTER 3: A THRONE IN FLAMES

The desert wind howled through the shattered streets of Jerusalem, carrying with it the acrid scent of smoke and blood. Herod's breath came in short, sharp bursts as he surveyed the ruins of the city from atop his horse. The Parthians had left a scar on Judea—a land already fractured by its own internal strife. Behind him, the remnants of his loyal forces gathered, their faces a tapestry of exhaustion and despair. They were fewer now, their ranks decimated by the siege, and their morale hung by a thread.

Herod's knuckles whitened as he gripped the reins. This was not defeat. It was a setback, a crucible from which he would emerge stronger. But first, he had to survive. The Parthian forces were relentless, sweeping through Judea like locusts, leaving death and chaos in their wake. Herod had been forced to abandon his stronghold, Masada, and now even Jerusalem was beyond saving. The only path left was one that led west—to Rome.

"We cannot hold this ground," Herod said, his voice sharp and resolute. His commanders exchanged uneasy glances but dared not argue. They had learned that Herod's decisions, however ruthless, were often the only thing keeping them alive.

The journey to Rome was fraught with peril. Herod traveled with a small retinue, navigating hostile territories and treacherous seas. At night, as they camped under the cold light of the stars, Herod's mind churned with plans and possibilities. The betrayal of the Hasmoneans, the relentless advance of the Parthians, the fracturing loyalty of his people—all of it fanned the flames of his ambition. He would not allow his enemies to write the story of his defeat. If the gods willed it, he would carve his name into the annals of history with blood and stone.

By the time Herod reached Rome, he was a man on the edge—physically battered but mentally unyielding. The grandeur of the Eternal City was both a balm and a challenge. Here, power flowed like the Tiber, and those who could harness it ruled the world. Herod knew he had to impress not only with words but with the force of his vision.

The Senate chamber was a theater of ambition. The air hummed with the murmurs of senators, their togas draped in folds that signified wealth and influence. At the center of it all stood Mark Antony, his presence commanding, and Octavian, whose youth belied the sharpness of his intellect. Herod's audience with the two most powerful men in the world was both an opportunity and a test.

"Herod of Judea," Mark Antony said, his voice resonating through the chamber. "You stand before us seeking Rome's favor. Speak your case."

Herod stepped forward, his spine straight despite the weight of his journey. "Honored senators, noble Antony, revered Octavian," he began, his voice steady and deliberate. "Judea stands as a gateway between Rome and the East, a land of strategic importance. But it is a land in turmoil. The Parthians have ravaged our cities, and internal divisions threaten to tear us apart."

He paused, letting his words sink in. "I come to you not as a supplicant but as a partner. Give me the authority to rule as King of the Jews, and I will restore order to Judea. I will ensure that the Parthians do not breach your western borders, and I will govern in a manner that brings glory to Rome."

Mark Antony leaned back, his expression contemplative. "You speak with conviction, Herod. But why should we trust you? You are an Idumean by birth, not of royal blood."

Herod met Antony's gaze without flinching. "Because I am not bound by the petty squabbles of dynasties. My loyalty is to Rome, and my ambition is aligned with yours. The Hasmoneans have failed you. Let me succeed where they could not."

Octavian, silent until now, leaned forward. His eyes were calculating, weighing Herod like a piece of gold on a scale. "And if we grant you this kingship, what guarantees do we have of your loyalty?"

Herod's lips curved into a faint smile. "My actions will speak louder than any promise. Allow me to prove myself, and you will find no ruler more devoted to Rome's cause."

The chamber fell silent, the weight of the moment hanging in the air. Finally, Antony nodded. "Very well. Let it be known that Herod of Judea is declared King of the Jews, by decree of the Roman Senate."

A ripple of murmurs spread through the chamber as Herod bowed deeply. Inside, his heart thundered with triumph. The throne he had envisioned was now within reach, but he knew the road ahead would be steep and fraught with danger.

Herod's return to Judea was a march of fire and steel. Backed by Roman forces, he set about reclaiming the territory lost to the Parthians. The campaign was brutal, a series of calculated strikes that left no room for mercy. Villages suspected of harboring Parthian sympathizers were razed, their inhabitants scattered or executed. Herod's name became both a rallying cry for his allies and a curse on the lips of his enemies.

CHAPTER 4: THE SIEGE OF JERUSALEM

The air above Jerusalem hung heavy with the smoke of siege fires, casting a blood-red haze over the once-proud city. From Herod's vantage point on the ridge, he could see the sprawling walls marred by the relentless assault of his war machines. Mangonels hurled stones with deafening thuds, their impacts tearing into the ancient stone defenses like thunder on dry earth. Below, his army encircled the city like a serpent tightening its grip, cutting off all supplies and hope of escape.

Herod's eyes narrowed as he scanned the walls for signs of weakness. The defenders, remnants of Parthian forces and Judean insurgents, were tenacious, their resistance bolstered by desperation. His lips pressed into a thin line. Desperation made men dangerous, but it also made them reckless. He would exploit both.

"My lord," his captain said, approaching with a salute. "The northern gate is holding, but the western wall... it's beginning to crumble."

Herod's gaze flicked to the western wall, where plumes of dust rose with each strike of his battering rams. "Double the rams," he said, his voice calm but edged with steel. "Break through by nightfall. Spare no one who stands in our way."

The captain hesitated, a flicker of doubt crossing his face. "And the civilians, my lord? Many have taken refuge inside the city."

Herod's jaw tightened. Civilians. Innocents. Words that had lost their meaning in the face of survival and ambition. "Jerusalem belongs to those strong enough to hold it," he said coldly. "If they resist, they are not innocent."

The captain bowed and departed; his footsteps swallowed by the din of war. Herod's gaze returned to the city, his mind a maelstrom of calculations. Each decision, each life taken, was a step closer to securing his throne. But somewhere beneath the layers of resolve, a faint echo stirred—the memory of Jerusalem as it had been a city of light and devotion, the crown jewel of Judea. He crushed the thought as quickly as it surfaced. Sentiment had no place here.

Inside the city, Mariamne stood in the shadow of the Temple Mount, her heart pounding with a mixture of fear and fury. The streets were chaos, filled with the cries of the wounded and the desperate prayers of those clinging to hope. Smoke curled into the air, blotting out the sun, as Herod's forces pressed closer. She had seen the battering rams splinter the gates, heard the relentless pounding of the siege engines. Each strike felt like a blow to her own soul.

Her family—her mother, Alexandra, and her younger brother Aristobulus—huddled in the relative safety of the Hasmonean quarter. But Mariamne had ventured out, unable to bear the suffocating tension of waiting. She walked among the people, her presence drawing whispers and reverent gazes. The Hasmonean princess, they called her. A symbol of a dynasty that once ruled Judea with divine favor. But what did that mean now, in the face of Herod's ruthless ascent?

"Princess," an old woman called out, clutching a child to her chest. "Will the Lord save us?"

Mariamne's throat tightened. She wanted to offer reassurance, to invoke the strength of her ancestors, but the words caught like thorns. She had seen Herod's armies. She had seen the fire in his eyes. And she knew that salvation would not come.

"Have faith," she said finally, though the words felt hollow. The woman nodded, her eyes brimming with tears, and Mariamne turned away, guilt and helplessness gnawing at her resolve.

As night fell, the final assault began. Herod stood at the forefront, clad in bronze armor that caught the flickering light of the siege fires. His sword gleamed in his hand, an extension of his will. He led the charge through the western breach, his voice cutting through the chaos as he commanded his men forward.

"Take the walls! Push them back! Show no mercy!"

The clash of steel on steel filled the air, mingling with the screams of the dying. Herod fought with a precision and ferocity that inspired both awe and fear. His blade cut down enemies with ruthless efficiency, each strike a testament to his determination. Around him, his soldiers surged like a tide, overwhelming the defenders with sheer force.

The streets of Jerusalem became a battlefield, their stones slick with blood. Herod's forces advanced relentlessly, driving the defenders back toward the Temple Mount. The sacred ground became a final bastion, its courtyards filled with those who refused to surrender. Herod's eyes burned as he approached, his steps measured, his resolve unshaken.

"Open the gates," he commanded, his voice echoing across the courtyard. "Kneel, and I will spare your lives."

The defenders hesitated, their faces etched with exhaustion and despair. But one man stepped forward, his sword raised defiantly. "We kneel to no king but the Lord!" he cried.

Herod's expression hardened. "Then you will die for a lost cause."

With a nod, he signaled his archers. A volley of arrows darkened the sky, their sharp points finding their marks with deadly precision. The defiant man fell, his body crumpling to the ground. The gates were breached moments later, and Herod's forces poured in, securing the Temple Mount.

When the city finally fell silent, it was a hollow victory. Herod stood at the center of the Temple courtyard, his armor spattered with blood, his sword heavy in his hand. Around him, the remnants of his army gathered, their faces grim. The city was his, but at what cost?

Mariamne watched from a distance, her heart breaking at the sight of the man who had taken everything she held dear. Herod, the man who now claimed to be the savior of Judea, stood amid the ruins of its holiest city. She felt a surge of anger, a burning resentment that threatened to consume her. This was the man her family had allied with, the man who now sought to rebuild his kingdom on the ashes of her people.

In the days that followed, Herod began the arduous task of restoring order to Jerusalem. He ordered the dead to be buried, the rubble cleared, and the fires extinguished. But even as the city began to heal, the scars of the siege remained—etched into its stones, its people, and Herod himself.

One evening, as the sun dipped below the horizon, Herod climbed to the top of the western wall. From there, he could see the expanse of the city, its broken silhouette softened by the golden light. For a moment, he allowed himself to breathe, to feel the weight of his actions settle on his shoulders.

"You've won," a voice said behind him. He turned to see Mariamne, her figure framed by the fading light. Her expression was unreadable, her tone sharp.

"Victory is a heavy burden," Herod replied, his voice quieter than she expected.

"And yet you carry it so easily," she said, her words cutting like glass. "Do you ever question the cost of your ambition?"

Herod's gaze met hers, and for a moment, something flickered in his eyes—regret, perhaps, or doubt. But it was gone as quickly as it had appeared.

"A kingdom cannot be built without sacrifice," he said finally. "You of all people should understand that."

Mariamne's jaw tightened. "A kingdom built on ashes will not stand."

Herod turned back to the city, his expression unreadable. "Then I will rebuild it with stone."

As the night enveloped Jerusalem, the city's fate hung in the balance, its future shaped by a man whose ambition knew no bounds and a woman who saw the cost of his rise more clearly than he ever could.

CHAPTER 5: THE MARRIAGE OF CONVENIENCE

The palace in Jerusalem was alive with preparation. Tapestries woven with golden threads hung from the walls, reflecting the flickering light of countless oil lamps. The air carried the fragrance of frankincense, mingling with the aroma of roasted lamb and spiced wine. Courtiers moved through the grand hall like shadows, their voices hushed but their eyes gleaming with anticipation. Tonight was a night of celebration —the union of Herod the Great and Mariamne, a marriage that would seal the fragile bond between the Idumean king and the Hasmonean dynasty.

Herod stood in his chambers, the weight of his new robes pressing down on his shoulders like the burden of his reign. The fabric was rich, crimson and gold, the colors of power. Yet, as he stared into the polished bronze mirror before him, he felt a pang of unease. This marriage was a calculated move, a strategic alliance to legitimize his rule in the eyes of Judea. But beneath the veneer of political necessity, there was something else—a yearning he could not quite name, a hope that Mariamne might see him as more than the ambitious man who had claimed her family's legacy.

"Your Majesty," a voice interrupted. Herod turned to see his trusted advisor, Nicolas of Damascus, standing at the doorway. The man's sharp eyes flickered with approval as he took in Herod's appearance. "The guests have gathered. It is time."

Herod nodded, his jaw tightening. "Let us begin."

The wedding ceremony was a grandeur spectacle. The hall was filled with the elite of Judea, their garments shimmering under the glow of hundreds of lamps. Priests chanted blessings in solemn tones, their voices weaving a tapestry of sacred tradition. At the center of it all stood Mariamne, her beauty luminous and arresting. Her gown, a flowing white adorned with silver embroidery, caught the light with every movement. Her dark eyes, framed by delicate features, were unreadable as she approached the altar.

Herod watched her intently, his chest tightening as she drew closer. There was strength in her bearing, a quiet defiance that both intrigued and unsettled him. When their eyes met, he offered a faint smile, but Mariamne's expression remained guarded.

The High Priest stepped forward, his voice ringing out over the assembly. "By this union, may Judea find peace and strength. Let the house of Herod and the house of Hasmonean stand united, as one family, under one God."

As the vows were exchanged, Herod's voice was firm, each word a pledge not only to Mariamne but to the vision he held for his kingdom. Mariamne's voice, by contrast, was steady but distant, as if the words were a script she had memorized rather than a promise she embraced.

When the ceremony ended and the hall erupted in applause, Herod took Mariamne's hand. Her fingers were cool against his palm, her grip light but unyielding. Together, they turned to face the crowd, the image of unity. But in the quiet space between their clasped hands, an unspoken tension lingered.

The feast that followed was a cacophony of sound and color. Musicians played lively tunes on lyres and flutes, while servants moved through the crowd bearing trays of delicacies. Herod sat at the head of the long table, Mariamne beside him, their thrones raised slightly above the rest. He glanced at her often, searching her face for some sign of emotion. But Mariamne remained composed, her gaze sweeping over the guests like a queen surveying her court.

"You look beautiful tonight," Herod said softly, leaning toward her.

Mariamne turned to him, her eyes meeting his with a calm that bordered on cold. "Thank you, my lord," she replied, her tone polite but devoid of warmth.

Herod's smile faltered. He leaned back, lifting his goblet to his lips to hide his unease. Around them, the courtiers laughed and toasted, oblivious to the undercurrent of tension between the newlyweds.

Later that night, when the halls had emptied and the echoes of music had faded, Herod and Mariamne found themselves alone in their chambers. The room was grand, its walls adorned with intricate mosaics and its air heavy with the scent of myrrh. A fire crackled in the hearth, casting flickering shadows that danced across the polished marble floor.

Mariamne stood near the window, her back to Herod, as she gazed out at the city. The soft light of the moon bathed her in an ethereal glow, making her seem almost otherworldly. Herod watched her in silence, his mind a whirlwind of thoughts. He had faced armies, sieges, and betrayals, yet in this moment, he felt unsteady, unsure of how to bridge the chasm between them.

"Mariamne," he said finally, his voice quieter than he intended. She turned, her expression unreadable.

"Yes, my lord?"

Herod hesitated, searching for the right words. "I know this marriage was not of your choosing. But I hope... I hope that, in time, you will come to see me as more than a king."

Mariamne's gaze softened, but only slightly. "And how do you see me, my lord? As a wife? Or as a pawn in your game of power?"

Herod's jaw tightened. "I see you as both. But more than that, I see you as a partner. Someone who can help me shape the future of this kingdom."

Mariamne stepped closer, her eyes searching his face. "You speak of partnership, yet it was your armies that brought this city to its knees. It was your sword that spilled the blood of my people. Tell me, Herod, how can I trust a man who conquers with one hand and offers marriage with the other?"

Herod's chest tightened, her words cut deeper than any blade. "Because I had no choice," he said, his voice low but firm. "Everything I have done has been for survival. For the future. For us."

Mariamne's eyes hardened. "Then I will trust you, my lord, when your actions prove your words."

In the weeks that followed, the marriage of Herod and Mariamne became the subject of both admiration and scrutiny. The union was celebrated as a symbol of unity, a blending of Idumean ambition and Hasmonean heritage. But behind the closed doors of the palace, the cracks in their relationship began to show.

Herod, consumed by the demands of ruling a fractured kingdom, often found himself drawn away from Mariamne. His days were filled with meetings, decrees, and the ever-present specter of Rome's expectations. Yet, in the quiet hours of the night, his thoughts often returned to her—to the way her gaze could pierce through his carefully constructed facade, to the quiet strength she carried even in the face of his power.

Mariamne, for her part, navigated the palace with the grace of a queen but the wariness of a captive. She maintained her composure in public, fulfilling her duties with poise, but in private, she wrestled with the weight of her new reality. Herod's ambition was a force of nature, and she feared being swept away by it.

One evening, as they dined together in the intimacy of their chambers, Herod reached for her hand. "Tell me what troubles you," he said, his voice uncharacteristically gentle.

Mariamne hesitated; her gaze fixed on the flickering candle between them. "I wonder, my lord, if you see this kingdom as your child or your prisoner."

Herod frowned, her words striking a nerve. "I see it as my responsibility. My legacy."

Mariamne met his eyes, her expression unreadable. "Then I hope, for all our sakes, that you can be a just father to it."

Herod's grip on her hand tightened for a moment before he released it, his mind churning with her words. In Mariamne, he saw a mirror of his own doubts, a reflection of the questions he could not afford to ask himself. And yet, he could not deny the pull she had on him—a force that was both a comfort and a challenge.

CHAPTER 6: ARCHITECT OF AMBITION

The first light of dawn bathed Jerusalem in a pale, golden glow, softening the jagged scars left by war. Herod stood atop the Temple Mount, his cloak billowing in the crisp morning air. Before he stretched the remnants of Solomon's Temple, its once-grand walls reduced to rubble by centuries of conquest and neglect. The air carried a faint chill, laced with the scent of dust and the distant murmur of the city waking below.

To Herod, the ruin was not a monument to the past but a foundation for his future. The Temple would rise again, grander than it had ever been, a testament to his reign and an offering to the God of his people. Yet, in his heart, the project was more than an act of devotion; it was a declaration of his legitimacy, a symbol of power to silence the whispers that still questioned his right to rule.

"Imagine it," Herod said, his voice carrying a rare note of awe. "Columns of marble reaching toward the heavens, gates adorned with gold and silver, courtyards wide enough to hold all of Judea in prayer."

Nicolas of Damascus, ever at his side, nodded approvingly. "It will be a wonder of the world, my lord. Future generations will speak of Herod's Temple with reverence."

Herod turned to his advisor, his expression hardening. "It must be perfect, Nicolas. Every stone must proclaim my vision, my authority. This Temple will stand as proof that I am not a usurper, but a king chosen by God and Rome alike."

Nicolas inclined his head. "Then let us begin, my king."

The announcement of Herod's grand plan sent ripples through Judea. Priests whispered of sacrilege, fearing that the Temple's reconstruction might defile its sanctity. Commoners debated in the markets, torn between awe at Herod's ambition and resentment over the burden it would place upon them. For the laborers who built it, the project was both a promise of work and a harbinger of hardship.

Among them was Yoram, a stonemason whose hands bore the calluses of years spent shaping stone. He stood in the shadow of the Mount, gazing up at the ruins with a mixture of reverence and dread. Around him, other workers gathered, their voices low as they spoke of the king's decree.

"He's rebuilding the Temple," one man said, his tone laced with skepticism. "But at what cost? We'll be breaking our backs for years, and for what? Another monument to his pride?"

Yoram remained silent, his gaze fixed on the crumbled walls. He had grown up hearing stories of Solomon's Temple, of its splendor and the divine presence that had once dwelled within. To rebuild it was an honor, but he could not ignore the weight of the task ahead. The king's ambition was boundless, and ambition, Yoram knew, often demanded sacrifice.

The construction began with a frenzy of activity. Herod's architects and engineers descended upon the site, their voices ringing out as they directed laborers to clear rubble and lay new foundations. Massive blocks of limestone were quarried and hauled to the Mount, their weight a testament to the enormity of Herod's vision. The clang of chisels against stone and the groan of wooden pulleys filled the air, a symphony of toil that echoed across the city.

Herod visited the site daily, his presence a mixture of inspiration and intimidation. He moved among the workers, his eyes sharp as he inspected their progress. To some, his visits were a source of pride; to others, a reminder of the immense pressure to meet his exacting standards.

"Faster," Herod barked one morning, his voice cutting through the din. "The eastern wall must be complete before the rains begin. There is no room for error."

Yoram, working near the base of the wall, felt the king's gaze linger on him. He straightened, his hands tightening around his chisel. Herod's presence was suffocating, a constant reminder that failure was not an option.

As the weeks turned into months, the Temple began to take shape. Columns of white marble rose toward the sky, their surfaces polished to a gleaming finish. The courtyards expanded, their sheer size dwarfing the laborers who toiled within them. Herod watched it all with a mixture of pride and impatience, his mind constantly racing ahead to the final result.

But beneath the grandeur lay a simmering tension. The priests, wary of Herod's Roman ties, questioned his motives. The common people, burdened by taxes and conscripted labor, whispered of rebellion. Even among Herod's court, there were murmurs of dissent, voices that questioned whether his ambition would ultimately consume him.

One evening, as Herod stood atop the nearly completed western wall, Mariamne joined him. The city stretched out below them, its lights flickering like stars fallen to earth. For a moment, the silence between them was peaceful, almost tender.

"It is beautiful," Mariamne said, her voice soft. "But at what cost,

Herod?"

Herod's jaw tightened. "Everything worth building demands sacrifice. The Temple will unite Judea, give our people a symbol of hope and strength."

Mariamne turned to him, her eyes searching for his face. "And does it give you hope? Or does it simply remind you of what you must prove?"

Herod's chest tightened, her words striking a nerve he had tried to bury. "You see doubt where there is none," he said, his tone clipped. "This Temple will stand long after we are gone. It will be my legacy."

Mariamne's gaze lingered on him; her expression unreadable. "I hope, for your sake, that legacy is enough."

For Yoram and the other laborers, the toll of the project was unrelenting. Days stretched into nights; the work as grueling as it was ceaseless. Injuries were common, and the specter of death loomed over the site like a shadow. Yet, even amid their suffering, there were moments of camaraderie, of shared purpose. The Temple was not just Herod's dream; it had become their burden, their creation.

One afternoon, as Yoram worked to carve an intricate design into a block of limestone, he paused to wipe the sweat from his brow. Around him, other workers labored in silence, their movements heavy with exhaustion. Yet, when he looked up at the rising walls, he felt a flicker of something he could not quite name. Pride, perhaps. Or defiance.

"It will be magnificent," he said quietly, more to himself than anyone else.

A fellow laborer nearby snorted. "Magnificent for the king, maybe. For us, it's just another weight on our backs."

Yoram didn't respond. He turned back to his work, his chisel striking the stone with renewed determination. Whatever the cost, this Temple would stand. And in its stones, Yoram would leave a mark that no king could erase.

As the first phase of the Temple's reconstruction neared completion, Herod gathered his court to witness the progress. The golden gates gleamed in the sunlight, their surfaces etched with intricate designs that seemed to catch the light and hold it captive. The courtyards stretched wide and open, their marble floors reflecting the azure sky above. It was a sight that stole the breath of even Herod's harshest critics.

"Behold," Herod said, his voice resonating across the crowd. "The Temple of Jerusalem, reborn. A symbol of our strength, our faith, and our future."

The assembled courtiers erupted to applause, their voices a symphony of praise. Yet, as Herod basked in their adulation, a shadow flickered across his mind. The cost of the Temple—not just in coin but in lives, in loyalty—was a weight he could not ignore. And though he stood at the pinnacle of his ambition, he could not shake the fear that it might all come crashing down.

That night, as Herod walked the empty halls of the palace, he found himself drawn back to the Temple Mount. The city was quiet, its streets bathed in the silver light of the moon. He stood before the unfinished structure, his eyes tracing the lines of the walls, the columns, the gates.

For a moment, he allowed himself to feel the enormity of what he had created. The Temple was not just a building; it was a statement, a defiance of time and doubt. Yet, in its shadow, Herod felt the creeping tendrils of uncertainty. He had built this Temple to prove his legitimacy, to silence the voices that questioned him. But as the wind whispered through the courtyards, he wondered if it would ever be enough.

CHAPTER 7: SEEDS OF BETRAYAL

The heavy air of the palace was thick with whispers. Jerusalem, still basking in the glow of Herod's grand plans, now found itself cloaked in intrigue. Alexandra moved through the halls like a shadow, her veil trailing behind her and her sharp eyes scanning every face. She had grown adept at reading the subtle shifts in power, the unspoken alliances that determined survival in Herod's court. And now, she saw an opportunity—a crack in the facade of Herod's seemingly unshakable rule.

Her daughter, Mariamne, was the key.

Alexandra found Mariamne in her chambers, standing by the latticed window that overlooked the Temple Mount. The newly risen walls gleamed in the sunlight, but Mariamne's gaze was distant, her thoughts elsewhere. She turned when her mother entered, her expression softening momentarily before hardening again—a reflex born of years of distrust.

"You shouldn't be here," Mariamne said, her voice quiet but firm. "If Herod finds us speaking like this, he will suspect something."

Alexandra smiled, a thin, calculated expression. "My dear, Herod already suspects everything. That is his nature. But we cannot allow his paranoia to dictate our lives."

Mariamne sighed, turning back to the window. "What do you want, Mother?"

Alexandra stepped closer, her voice lowering to a conspiratorial tone. "You are his queen. You share his bed, his secrets. But you are more than that, Mariamne. You are a Hasmonean. The blood of kings flows through your veins. Herod may claim the throne, but it is you who carries the true legacy of Judea."

Mariamne's hands tightened on the windowsill. "And what would you have me do? Defy him openly? That would be suicide."

Alexandra's expression softened, though her eyes gleamed with purpose. "I do not ask for defiance, only vigilance. Herod's rule is not as secure as he pretends. The people grumble under the weight of his taxes, the priests question his motives, and Rome... Rome is ever watchful. If the time comes when his grip falters, you must be ready to act. For your children, for our family."

Mariamne turned to face her mother; her expression conflicted. "Do you not see what this marriage has cost me? I am his queen, but I am also his prisoner. To defy him would be to risk everything."

Alexandra placed a hand on Mariamne's shoulder, her voice soft but insistent. "And to do nothing would be to lose everything. Remember who you are, my daughter. Remember the strength of our blood."

Herod felt the shift before he saw it. The subtle tension in Mariamne's voice, the guarded look in her eyes, the way her words seemed chosen with great care. It unsettled him, gnawed at the edges of his thoughts even as he buried himself in the work of rebuilding his kingdom.

One evening, as they dined together in the privacy of their chambers, he studied her closely. The firelight played across her features, casting her in warm tones that belied the cool distance he now felt.

"You have been quiet lately," Herod said, his tone light but probing.

"Is something troubling you?"

Mariamne looked up from her plate, her expression calm but unreadable. "The weight of the crown, perhaps. It is not an easy thing to bear."

Herod's lips curved into a faint smile. "You wear it well. The people adore you, and you give them hope."

"And you?" Mariamne asked, her gaze steady. "Do you adore me, Herod? Or do you simply see me as a piece in your game of power?"

Herod's smile faltered, the question striking closer to the truth than he cared to admit. He reached for his goblet, taking a slow sip of wine to buy himself time. "I see you as my queen," he said finally. "My partner in all things."

Mariamne's lips twitched, almost as if she were about to smile, but the moment passed. "Then I hope your faith in me is well-placed, my king."

The court buzzed with rumors. Whispers of Alexandra's ambitions reached Herod's ears, carried by spies who lurked in the shadows of every corridor. He dismissed some as mere gossip, but others struck a chord of unease. Alexandra had always been a thorn in his side, her Hasmonean pride a constant reminder of the fragility of his alliance with Mariamne.

One night, unable to sleep, Herod summoned Nicolas of Damascus to his chambers. The advisor entered quietly, his sharp eyes immediately noting the tension in Herod's stance.

"You are troubled, my lord," Nicolas said, his voice carefully neutral.

Herod paced the room, his hands clasped behind his back. "Alexandra. I have tolerated her schemes for the sake of peace, but now I fear she may be poisoning Mariamne against me."

Nicolas's brow furrowed. "Mariamne is loyal, my king. She has shown no signs of rebellion."

"Not openly," Herod said, his voice low and sharp. "But there is a distance between us now, a barrier I cannot breach. If Alexandra is behind it, she must be dealt with."

Nicolas hesitated. "And what of Mariamne? How will she react if you move against her mother?"

Herod's jaw tightened. "That is what stays my hand. But if Alexandra pushes me further, I will have no choice."

Mariamne's suspicions of Herod's growing distrust were confirmed one morning when she found her chambers being searched. The servants, normally deferential and quiet, now moved with nervous urgency under the watchful eyes of Herod's guards. Herod himself was not present, but his absence only made the intrusion more glaring.

She stood in the center of the room, her posture regal and unyielding, as the guards rifled through her belongings. "Is this how a king treats his queen?" she demanded, her voice cold.

One of the guards hesitated, his gaze flickering with guilt, but he said nothing. When they finally left, Mariamne sat by the window, her hands trembling with a mixture of anger and fear. Herod's mistrust was growing, and she knew that Alexandra's machinations had only stoked the flames.

When Herod returned that evening, Mariamne confronted him. "You sent your guards to search my chambers," she said, her voice steady but edged with fury. "Do you think I would betray you, Herod? After all I have sacrificed?"

Herod's expression was unreadable, his eyes dark and searching. "I think loyalty is a fragile thing," he said after a long pause. "And I think Alexandra's ambitions make her dangerous. If you are caught in her web, I must know."

Mariamne's chest tightened, her anger flaring. "I am your wife, not your enemy. But if you treat me as the latter, you will make it so."

Herod stepped closer, his voice dropping to a whisper. "You are my queen, Mariamne. But never forget that queens have fallen before."

Their eyes locked, the tension between them crackling like a storm. In that moment, Mariamne saw not the man she had once hoped to love, but a king consumed by paranoia and ambition. And Herod saw not his queen, but a woman whose loyalty he could no longer take for granted.

The seeds of betrayal had been sown, and though neither Herod nor Mariamne could yet see the harvest, both felt its weight. The palace, once a place of uneasy harmony, is now pulsed with suspicion and fear. And in the shadows, Alexandra watched, her mind ever calculating, her ambitions undimmed.

CHAPTER 8: A HIGH PRIEST'S DEATH

The summer heat clung to Jerusalem like an oppressive shroud, filling the palace halls with a stifling stillness that mirrored the growing tension within. Herod stood at the edge of the palace gardens; his eyes fixed on the figure of Aristobulus III as the young man walked beside the reflecting pool. The high priest's white robes gleamed in the midday sun, a stark contrast to the dark clouds gathering in Herod's mind.

Aristobulus was a threat. Herod's every instinct screamed it. The boy, though barely seventeen, carried the undeniable charisma of a Hasmonean prince. The people adored him, their whispers of hope growing louder with each passing day. They called him "God's chosen," a living reminder of the dynasty Herod had sought to bury. It was a danger Herod could not afford to ignore.

Nicolas of Damascus approached, his sandals crunching softly against the gravel. "The people's affection for Aristobulus grows by the day," he said, his voice carefully neutral.

Herod's jaw tightened. "Affection can be weaponized. The boy's mere presence is enough to undermine my rule. Alexandra knows this; she placed him on the altar for that very purpose."

Nicolas hesitated. "He is young, my king. Perhaps his influence can be contained."

Herod turned to face his advisor, his eyes cold and unyielding. "Containment is a risk I cannot take. The priests whisper his name in reverence, the people see him as their savior. If I let this continue, it will be my crown that is toppled."

There was a long silence, broken only by the faint ripple of water in the reflecting pool.

"Then what must be done?" Nicolas asked softly.

Herod's gaze returned to Aristobulus, now kneeling to cup water in his hands. "The people will mourn him," Herod said, his voice low and hard. "But they will not revolt if it looks like an accident."

The banquet that evening was a spectacle of opulence, designed to dazzle and distract. Musicians played lively melodies on lyres and flutes, while servants carried platters of roasted meats and fine wines to the guests. Aristobulus sat near the center of the table, his youthful face lit with a radiant smile as he spoke with Mariamne.

Mariamne watched her brother with quiet pride, her heart lifting at the sight of his joy. She had always been fiercely protective of Aristobulus, seeing in him a glimpse of the past glory their family had once known. But as her gaze shifted to Herod, seated at the head of the table, a sense of unease crept over her. His expression was composed, almost genial, but there was a tension in his posture, a darkness lurking behind his eyes.

When the feast ended, Herod suggested a diversion. "The heat has been relentless," he said, his tone light. "Let us cool ourselves in the palace pool. A bit of sport to ease the evening."

Aristobulus hesitated, glancing at Mariamne, who gave him a small, reassuring nod. "That sounds delightful," the young priest said, rising from his seat.

The pool shimmered under the moonlight, its surface reflecting the pale glow of the stars. Herod and his companions entered the water with laughter and splashes, the tension of the evening dissolved into the illusion of camaraderie. Aristobulus joined them, his youthful exuberance drawing smiles from those around him.

But Herod's laughter was hollow, his smiles forced. As the sport continued, he moved closer to Aristobulus, his heart pounding with a mixture of fear and resolve. The boy was too dangerous to live. His death would secure Herod's throne, silence the whispers of dissent, and remind those who dared challenge him of the cost of defiance.

At a signal from Herod, two of his trusted guards approached under the guise of play. They grabbed Aristobulus, pushing him beneath the water. The boy struggled, his movements frantic, his hands clawing at the surface as the guards held him down.

Herod watched, his face a mask of detachment. The ripples in the water grew violent, then subsided, leaving the pool eerily still. The guards released their grip, stepping back as Aristobulus's lifeless body floated to the surface.

For a moment, no one moved. The laughter had ceased, replaced by a heavy silence that pressed down on the gathered men. Herod forced himself to speak, his voice calm but tinged with feigned shock. "A tragedy," he said. "The boy was too bold in his play. The water claimed him before we could act."

The words tasted like ash in his mouth.

When Mariamne heard the news, the world seemed to tilt beneath her feet. She rushed to the pool, her breath coming in short gasps as she saw her brother's body being pulled from the water. The sight of his still, pale face tore a scream from her throat, a sound that echoed through the palace like a mourning bell.

Herod approached her cautiously, his expression grave. "Mariamne," he began, his voice soft. "It was an accident. A terrible loss for us all."

Mariamne's head snapped toward him, her eyes blazing with fury. "An accident?" she spat. "Do not insult me with lies, Herod. I see your hand in this. You could not bear his light, his innocence, so you snuffed it out."

Herod's expression darkened, a flicker of anger breaking through his mask of composure. "I did what I had to do to protect this kingdom," he said, his voice low and sharp. "Aristobulus was a threat, not just to me but to the stability of Judea. You may not see it now, but one day you will understand."

Mariamne stepped closer, her voice trembling with rage. "I will never understand. You have taken everything from me, Herod. My family, my freedom, and now my brother. You are not a king. You are a tyrant."

Herod's chest tightened, her words cut deeper than any blade. For a moment, he considered reaching for her, pleading with her to see his side, to understand the impossible choices he had been forced to make. But the look in her eyes stopped him. It was not anger alone that he saw there; it was hatred.

"I am what this kingdom needs," he said finally, his voice cold. "Whether you see it or not."

Mariamne turned away from him, her shoulders trembling with grief. She knelt beside Aristobulus's body, her hands gently brushing his damp hair from his forehead. Tears fell freely down her cheeks as she whispered a prayer, her words a quiet plea for justice.

Herod watched her in silence, his heart a tangle of regret and resolve. He had secured his throne, but in doing so, he had driven an even deeper wedge between himself and the woman he had once hoped would stand beside him. As he walked away, the sound of Mariamne's sobs followed him, haunting him like a ghost.

The death of Aristobulus sent shockwaves through Judea. The priests mourned the loss of their young high priest, their chants of lamentation filling the streets. The people whispered of foul play, their grief mingling with anger. And in the palace, Mariamne's silence spoke volumes, a wall of ice that Herod could not breach.

In the days that followed, Herod threw himself into his work, overseeing the construction of the Temple with a renewed intensity. But no amount of stone or gold could quiet the voice in his mind, the one that whispered of the boy's lifeless eyes, of the hatred in Mariamne's gaze.

He had built his kingdom on ambition, on sacrifice. But as he stood atop the Temple Mount, the city sprawling below him, he wondered how much more he would have to give—and how much he could take before it all came crashing down.

CHAPTER 9: THE ROMAN SHADOW

The streets of Rome pulsed with life, a cacophony of voices rising above the clatter of horse hooves and the grind of cartwheels on cobblestone. The Eternal City stood as a monument to power and ambition, its marble temples and sprawling forums glittering under the midday sun. Herod stepped off his gilded chariot, his finely embroidered cloak trailing behind him, and surveyed the scene with a mixture of admiration and unease. Here, in the heart of the Roman Empire, alliances were forged and lives unmade with the flick of a senator's quill.

He was no stranger to Rome, yet each visit reminded him of its paradox: a city both intoxicatingly grand and ruthlessly pragmatic. Today, his purpose was clear—to solidify his alliance with Augustus, the man whose favor secured his throne. But Herod knew that the shadow of doubt lingered over him, cast by whispers of his growing paranoia and the unrest in Judea.

"My king," Nicolas of Damascus murmured at his side. "The palace awaits. Augustus has granted you an audience this afternoon."

Herod nodded; his expression unreadable. "Let us not keep the emperor waiting."

The hall of Augustus was an architectural marvel, its vaulted ceiling adorned with frescoes depicting the triumphs of Rome. Columns of polished marble lined the space, their surfaces gleaming like water in the sunlight. Herod approached the dais with measured steps, his every movement calculated to project confidence.

Augustus sat on a simple but elevated throne, his tunic and cloak unadorned yet carrying an air of authority that needed no embellishment. His sharp eyes studied Herod with a mix of curiosity and calculation.

"Herod of Judea," Augustus said, his voice calm but firm. "Welcome to Rome. It has been some time since we last spoke."

Herod inclined his head, his tone deferential but steady. "Caesar, it is always an honor to stand before you. Judea thrives under your protection, and I am here to reaffirm my loyalty to Rome."

Augustus's lips curved into a faint smile. "Loyalty is a precious thing, especially in times of uncertainty. Tell me, Herod, how fares your kingdom?"

The question was simple, but Herod knew its weight. He chose his words carefully. "Judea is strong, but it is not without challenges. People cling to tradition, and there are factions that resist change. Yet, through Rome's support, we have achieved much. The Temple stands as a testament to our shared vision of prosperity."

Augustus nodded; his expression unreadable. "Your achievements are noted. But I have also heard troubling reports. Murmurs of unrest. Accusations of... instability. What do you say to these?"

Herod's jaw tightened, but he forced a smile. "Dissent is the language of the discontented, Caesar. Those who benefit from chaos will always seek to undermine order. I assure you, my rule is firm, and my loyalty to Rome unwavering."

Augustus leaned back, his gaze piercing. "I hope so, Herod. For both our sakes."

As Herod left the hall, the weight of the exchange settled heavily on him. Augustus's questions had been pointed; his approval measured. Herod knew that Rome's faith in him was not unconditional. He would need to prove, time and again, that he was a ruler worthy of their backing.

Later that evening, at a banquet held in his honor, Herod mingled with senators and envoys, his charm as polished as the silver goblets they held. Yet, even as he laughed and exchanged pleasantries, he could feel the eyes of one man on him—Lucius Calpurnius, a Roman envoy known for his shrewdness.

Lucius approached as the banquet waned, his expression friendly but his tone laced with curiosity. "King Herod, your reputation precedes you. Tell me, how does one balance the demands of Rome with the traditions of Judea?"

Herod smiled; his answer ready. "It is a delicate dance, but one I have learned well. Judea's traditions are its strength, but Rome's guidance ensures its future. My role is to harmonize the two."

Lucius raised an eyebrow. "A challenging task. I hear there are those who question your methods."

Herod's smile tightened. "Leadership often invites scrutiny. But my actions speak for themselves. Stability and prosperity are my priorities."

Lucius nodded, his gaze lingering on Herod for a moment longer before he turned away. The conversation, though brief, left Herod uneasy. Lucius's questions were polite, but they carried an undercurrent of doubt. It was a reminder that his every move was being watched.

Back in Jerusalem, the Roman shadow loomed large. Lucius, sent by Augustus to observe Herod's court, arrived with an entourage of scribes and soldiers. His presence was both a reassurance and a threat, a symbol of Rome's interest in Judea's affairs.

Herod welcomed Lucius with open arms, his hospitality flawless. Lavish feasts were held, tours of the Temple organized, and displays of Judea's prosperity orchestrated to impress. Yet, beneath the surface, cracks began to show.

In the marketplace, whispers of dissent grew louder. The common people, burdened by Herod's taxes and wary of Roman influence, spoke of their king with both awe and resentment. In the palace, tensions simmered among Herod's advisors, their loyalty tested by his growing paranoia.

Lucius observed it all with a practiced eye. He saw the grandeur of Herod's vision, but also the cost it exacted. The Temple, though magnificent, had been built on the backs of laborers whose faces bore the strain of endless toil. The court, though resplendent, was rife with intrigue and fear. And Herod himself, though charismatic, carried an air of volatility that Lucius found unsettling.

One evening, as Lucius dined with Herod and his court, he posed a question that silenced the room. "Tell me, King Herod, what legacy do you hope to leave?"

Herod set down his goblet, his expression thoughtful. "I wish to be remembered as a builder of greatness. A king who united his people and brought them prosperity. A man who ensured that Judea's light would shine for generations to come."

Lucius nodded, his gaze steady. "And at what cost?"

The question hung in the air, heavy with implication. Herod's eyes darkened, but he forced a smile. "Every great achievement demands sacrifice. History will judge whether the cost was worth it."

In the days that followed, Lucius's observations became more pointed. He spoke with priests, merchants, and laborers, gathering a mosaic of perspectives that painted a complex picture of Herod's reign. He saw the fear that lurked behind the courtiers' smiles, the exhaustion etched into the faces of the workers, the simmering unrest that threatened to boil over.

One afternoon, as Lucius toured the Temple Mount, he paused to speak with a stonemason named Yoram. The man's hands were calloused, his face weathered by years of labor.

"The Temple is a wonder," Lucius said, his tone conversational. "You must be proud to have contributed to it."

Yoram hesitated, his gaze flickering to the guards nearby. "It is a great work," he said carefully. "But greatness comes at a price."

Lucius studied him for a moment before nodding. "Indeed, it does."

When Lucius returned to Rome, he carried with him a report that was both glowing and cautionary. Herod's achievements were undeniable, his ambition unmatched. But the cracks in his rule were visible, even from the outside. Augustus read the report in silence, his expression betraying nothing.

"Herod is a capable king," Lucius concluded. "But his reign is built on a foundation of fear. Whether it will endure, only time will tell."

Augustus set the report aside, his thoughts turning to the man who ruled Judea in Rome's name. Herod was useful, yes, but he was also dangerous. And as the emperor stared out at the city that symbolized his own power, he wondered how long such a delicate balance could last.

CHAPTER 10: A KING'S FEARS

The flickering glow of the oil lamps cast long, restless shadows across the walls of Herod's private chamber. The king sat alone, hunched over a scroll of reports from his advisors. His fingers tapped the edge of the polished table, each tap echoing like the distant beat of a war drum. The silence in the room was oppressive, broken only by the faint rustle of the parchment as Herod's eyes darted across its contents.

The words blurred together, fragments of sentences gnawing at the edge of his mind: "Discontent in the northern provinces," "Increased murmurs among the Temple workers," "Potential alliances forming among disloyal factions." Each line seemed to pulse with treachery, feeding the dark specter that loomed ever larger in Herod's thoughts.

He pushed the scroll aside and rose abruptly, the chair scraping against the stone floor. The weight of his crown—a metaphor he had once dismissed as poetic indulgence—felt all too real now. Judea was his, carved out of chaos and held together by his iron will, but it was a kingdom riddled with cracks. And in those cracks, Herod saw betrayal.

The first signs of unrest came from the workers at the Temple.

It began quietly: whispered conversations in the shadows of the towering scaffolds, furtive glances exchanged as blocks of limestone were hauled into place. Yoram, the stonemason who had labored tirelessly on the Temple's grand walls, found himself at the heart of dissent. He had not sought leadership, but his words carried weight among the laborers, and their shared grievances gave them strength.

"We break our backs to build his legacy," one man said bitterly as they gathered in the dim light of a tallow candle. "And for what? Higher taxes? Empty promises?"

Yoram raised a hand to quiet the murmurs. His face, weathered by years of toil, was grim. "Herod's Temple is meant to stand as a monument to unity," he said. "But what unity is there when the people who build it are crushed beneath its weight?"

The men nodded, their eyes reflecting a mixture of anger and resolve. Yoram continued, his voice low but firm. "If we want to be heard, we must stand together. The king does not listen to whispers, but he will hear a roar."

In the palace, Herod's paranoia deepened. His court, once a place of calculated splendor, now felt like a stage for hidden plots. He saw betrayal in every smile, treachery in every deferential bow. Even his family was not exempt. Mariamne's silences, once a source of mystery and intrigue, now struck him as veiled defiance. Alexandra's sharp tongue and unyielding pride became weapons he imagined aimed at his back.

"My king," Nicolas of Damascus ventured cautiously one evening as they dined in the echoing expanse of the great hall. "Your concerns are valid, but I urge you to tread carefully. Mistrust can be as destructive as rebellion."

Herod's eyes narrowed, his fork paused mid-air. "Mistrust is the only thing that has kept this kingdom intact," he said coldly. "I built Judea on vigilance, Nicolas. Do not ask me to abandon it now."

Nicolas hesitated, then inclined his head. "As you wish, my king. But remember, fear can forge bonds, but it can also break them."

Herod said nothing, his gaze fixed on the table before him. His mind churned with Nicolas's words, even as he dismissed them. Fear had been his ally for so long that he could no longer see its cost.

In the weeks that followed, Herod tightened his grip on the kingdom. Spies were dispatched to infiltrate the Temple workforce, their task is to root out the source of the unrest. Soldiers patrolled the streets with increasing frequency, their presence a silent warning to those who might harbor rebellious thoughts. The people, once awed by Herod's ambition, now whispered of a tyrant whose paranoia threatened to consume him.

Yoram and his fellow laborers, aware of the growing danger, moved their meetings to more secluded places: the dark recess of the quarry, the abandoned wine cellars beneath the city. Their plans grew bolder, their numbers swelling with each passing day.

"If we stop working," Yoram said during one such gathering, "we halt the construction. The Temple is Herod's pride, his proof of legitimacy. Without it, his power wavers. That is where we strike."

The men nodded, their expressions a mixture of fear and determination. They knew the risks, but desperation had given them courage. For many, it was not just a matter of rebellion but survival.

Herod's suspicions reached a fever pitch when reports of the laborers' discontent reached his ears. He summoned his council to the palace, the room charged with tension as he paced before them.

"The Temple workers conspire against me," Herod said, his voice sharp. "They forget that their livelihood, their very lives, depend on my rule. I will remind them."

Nicolas, ever the voice of caution, spoke carefully. "My king, a heavy hand may silence dissent, but it will also breed resentment. Perhaps... dialogue might yield a better outcome."

Herod turned on him, his eyes blazing. "Dialogue?" he spat. "These men are traitors. They do not deserve dialogue; they deserve punishment."

The room fell silent, the weight of Herod's words hanging heavily in the air. His advisors exchanged uneasy glances, but none dared challenge him further.

Under the cover of darkness, Herod's soldiers descended upon the Temple Mount. The workers, roused from their makeshift sleeping quarters, were herded into the courtyards, their faces pale with fear. Torches cast flickering light on the massive stone walls, the flames dancing like specters of judgment.

Yoram stood among them, his heart pounding as the soldiers barked orders. He had known this moment would come, but the reality of it was more terrifying than he had imagined. Still, he held his ground, his jaw set in defiance.

Herod arrived moments later, his presence commanding and menacing. He surveyed the crowd, his expression a mask of cold fury.

"You forget your place," he said, his voice echoing through the courtyard. "You dare to conspire against your king? Against the man who has given you purpose?"

One of the workers stepped forward, his knees trembling but his voice steady. "We work, my lord, but we do not live. The burden you place on us is too great. We seek only fairness."

Herod's gaze hardened. "Fairness?" he repeated, his tone dripping with disdain. "You speak of fairness while you plot to undermine the very foundation of this kingdom. You will learn, as others have before you, that dissent is not tolerated in Judea."

He signaled to his guards, who seized the man and dragged him away. The crowd erupted in murmurs; their fear palpable.

Herod raised a hand for silence. "Let this serve as a warning. Continue your work or face the consequences."

The rebellion was crushed before it could fully take shape, but the scars it left on Herod's rule were deep. The workers returned to their tasks; their spirits broken but their resentment festering. In the palace, Herod's paranoia grew unchecked, poisoning even the moments of fleeting triumph.

One night, as he stood on the balcony overlooking the city, Mariamne joined him. She said nothing at first, her gaze fixed on the lights that dotted the streets below. When she finally spoke, her voice was quiet but firm.

"Fear is a poor foundation for a kingdom, Herod."

He turned to her, his expression guarded. "And what would you have me build it on? Love? Trust? Those are luxuries a king cannot afford."

Mariamne met his gaze, her eyes filled with a sadness that cut through him. "Perhaps not. But without them, you will rule a kingdom of shadows, where even your victories feel hollow."

Herod said nothing, his thoughts a tumult of anger, regret, and longing. As Mariamne turned and walked away, her words lingered in the air, a quiet echo of the doubts he could not silence.

And in the streets below, the seeds of rebellion lay dormant, waiting for the moment when fear alone would no longer be enough to hold them back.

CHAPTER 11: MARIAMNE'S TRIAL

The great hall of Herod's palace had never felt so oppressive. Its towering columns, carved with intricate depictions of Judea's history, seemed to loom over the gathered court, their stone faces impassive witnesses to the drama unfolding below. The air was heavy with the murmur of uneasy voices, a low hum that only ceased when Herod entered, his presence commanding the room into silence.

Mariamne stood at the center of the hall, her figure regal despite the chains that bound her wrists. Her dark eyes, defiant and unyielding, met Herod's from across the room. For a moment, the years of their marriage seemed to hang between them, a tapestry woven with moments of tenderness, ambition, and betrayal. But the thread of trust that had once bound them was frayed beyond repair.

Herod ascended the dais, his expression a mask of cold authority. Yet, beneath the surface, his mind churned with doubt and fury. The whispers of Mariamne's supposed infidelity had reached him like a poison, spreading through his thoughts until they consumed him. He had loved her once, but love had given way to suspicion, and suspicion to paranoia.

"Mariamne," Herod said, his voice echoing through the hall, "you stand accused of betraying your king and your marriage. What do you say to these charges?"

Mariamne's chin lifted, her voice clear and steady. "I say that these charges are born of your own fears, not of truth. I have been loyal to you, Herod, even when you did not deserve it. But your paranoia blinds you to everything but your own insecurities."

The court gasped at her boldness, a ripple of shock passing through the assembled courtiers. Herod's jaw tightened, his hands clenching the arms of his throne. "You dare speak to me in such a manner? After all I have done for you, for your family?"

Mariamne's gaze did not waver. "You speak of what you have done, but do you remember what you have taken? My brother, my peace, my freedom. And now you would take my honor as well. I will not let you."

The trial unfolded with a brutal inevitability. Witnesses were called, their testimonies carefully curated to paint Mariamne as a traitor. One by one, they spoke of clandestine meetings, of whispered words exchanged in shadowed corridors. The evidence was thin, a web of conjecture spun by Herod's spies, but in the charged atmosphere of the court, it was enough to sow doubt.

Among the witnesses was Salome, Herod's sister, whose rivalry with Mariamne had long been a source of tension. Her testimony was laced with venom, each word a dagger aimed at Mariamne's reputation.

"She has always thought herself above us," Salome said, her voice dripping with disdain. "Even as queen, she treated the court with disdain. And now we see the truth of her arrogance. She believed she could betray Herod and face no consequences."

Mariamne's lips tightened, but she held her silence. Herod watched her closely, searching for any sign of guilt, but her expression remained resolute.

From his seat in the shadows, Nicolas of Damascus observed

the trial with growing unease. He had served Herod for years, navigating the king's volatile moods and ruthless ambition, but this was different. The trial was not about justice; it was a spectacle, a performance designed to validate Herod's paranoia.

When Nicolas's turn came to speak, he chose his words carefully. "My king," he began, "I have served you loyally, and I will speak only the truth. I have seen no evidence to suggest that Mariamne has betrayed you. Her conduct has always been above reproach."

Herod's eyes narrowed; his tone sharp. "Are you saying the witnesses lie?"

"I am saying," Nicolas replied, his voice steady, "that we must be cautious. False accusations serve no one, least of all the crown."

Herod's gaze hardened, but he said nothing. Nicolas returned to his seat, his heart heavy with the knowledge that his words had likely fallen on deaf ears.

As the trial dragged on, Mariamne's defiance only seemed to fuel Herod's anger. He had expected tears, pleas for mercy, but instead, she stood tall, her dignity unshaken. It was both infuriating and disarming, a reminder of the strength that had drawn him to her in the first place.

Late into the night, after the court had been dismissed, Herod sat alone in his chamber, the echoes of the trial still ringing in his ears. He poured himself a goblet of wine, his hands trembling slightly as he lifted it to his lips. He had built his kingdom on ambition and vigilance, but now he wondered if he had sacrificed too much in the process. Mariamne's words haunted him, cutting through his defenses with brutal precision.

"You are not a king," she had said, "you are a man consumed by fear."

He slammed the goblet down, the wine spilling across the table like blood. Fear. The word burned in his mind, a reminder of the shadow that had followed him since his rise to power. Fear of betrayal, of failure, of losing everything he had fought to build.

The following day, the court reconvened for the verdict. Herod's advisors, sensing his mood, remained silent as he addressed the room. His voice was steady, but his eyes betrayed the turmoil within.

"Mariamne," he said, "you have been accused of infidelity and treachery. The evidence against you is troubling, but I will give you one final chance to defend yourself."

Mariamne stepped forward, her chains clinking softly with each movement. Her gaze swept across the court, lingering on Salome's smirk, Nicolas's worried frown, and finally, Herod's guarded expression.

"I have nothing more to say," she said, her voice calm. "You have already made your decision, Herod. I see it in your eyes. Do what you must, but know this: your paranoia will be your undoing."

Herod's jaw tightened, his hands clenching the arms of his throne. For a moment, the room was silent, the tension so thick it seemed to press against every breath. Then, with a wave of his hand, Herod pronounced the sentence.

"Mariamne is guilty of treachery," he said, his voice ringing out like a death knell. "She shall be executed."

A gasp rippled through the court, but Mariamne did not flinch. Herod rose from his throne, his gaze meeting her one last time. In her eyes, he saw no fear, but something far worse: contempt.

CHAPTER 12: THE EXECUTION

The morning sky was a muted gray, its clouds thick and unyielding, as if nature itself mourned what was to come. The city was hushed, its streets lined with somber faces, each one etched with disbelief and sorrow. From the high windows of the palace, Herod watched the preparations for Mariamne's execution unfold. The scaffold, stark and unadorned, rose in the center of the square like a cruel monument. His hands gripped the cold stone of the windowsill, the sharp edges digging into his flesh, but he did not move.

Mariamne stood at the heart of the square, her figure regal even in chains. The crowd parted as she walked toward the scaffold, their silence more piercing than any cry. Her dark hair flowed loose over her shoulders, a contrast to the starkness of her fate. She wore no finery, only a simple white gown, but there was dignity in her bearing that transcended her circumstances. Herod's breath caught as he saw her step forward, her head held high, her gaze unbroken.

From his perch, he could not hear the murmurs of the people, but he saw their faces. They adored her, even now. Perhaps more so now that she was about to be lost to them forever. The thought gnawed at him, a relentless specter that whispered of the price he had paid for his crown.

The executioner waited at the scaffold, his expression a mask of practiced indifference. Mariamne ascended the wooden steps without hesitation, her movements graceful, as though she were ascending a throne instead of her death. The crowd's eyes followed her every step, their collective grief palpable.

The High Priest, his voice trembling with the weight of the moment, stepped forward to deliver the final rites. "Mariamne, Queen of Judea, you stand condemned by the decree of your king. May your soul find peace beyond this world."

Mariamne turned her gaze to the palace balcony where Herod stood. Their eyes met across the distance, and for a moment, time seemed to pause. There was no fear in her expression, only a quiet resolve and a flicker of something that pierced him to his core—contempt, perhaps, or sorrow.

She said nothing as the executioner approached, her silence a final act of defiance. Herod's vision blurred as the blade was raised, the world narrowing to the singular, unbearable moment when it fell. The crowd erupted into cries of anguish as her body crumpled to the platform, but Herod heard nothing. The sound of the blade echoed in his mind, reverberating through the hollow spaces of his soul.

The hours after the execution passed in a haze. Herod wandered the halls of the palace, his steps aimless and unsteady. The faces of his advisors blurred together as they spoke to him in hushed tones, their words meaningless. He retreated to his private chamber, bolting the heavy doors behind him. Only in solitude could he face the enormity of what he had done.

The room was dark, lit only by the flickering light of a single lamp. Herod sank into a chair, his head in his hands, as the memories surged forward unbidden. He saw Mariamne as she had been in the early days of their marriage, her laughter ringing like music through the halls. He remembered the way she had looked at him then, with a mixture of curiosity and warmth, as though she had seen something in him worth believing in.

A memory surfaced, sharp and vivid. It was a quiet evening, years ago, when they had escaped the weight of the court to walk in the palace gardens. The scent of jasmine hung heavy in the air, and the distant murmur of the city was a soothing backdrop. They had paused by the fountain, its waters glimmering in the moonlight.

"Do you ever wish things were different?" Mariamne had asked, her voice soft.

Herod had looked at her, startled by the question. "Different how?"

She had turned to him, her dark eyes searching for his. "Simpler. Without the weight of crowns and kingdoms. Without the need for power."

Herod had laughed then, a low, bitter sound. "Power is not a choice, Mariamne. It is a necessity. Without it, we are nothing."

She smiled faintly, her gaze distant. "Perhaps. But sometimes I wonder if we lose more than we gain by chasing it."

He had said nothing, unable to find the words to bridge the chasm her question had opened. Instead, he had reached for her hand, and she had allowed him to take it. For a moment, they had stood in silence, the world narrowing to space between them.

The memory dissolved, leaving Herod gasping for air. He rose abruptly, pacing the room as if he could escape the ghosts that haunted him. But they were everywhere: in the stillness of the chamber, in the shadows that danced on the walls, in the lingering scent of jasmine that seemed to taunt him.

"You brought this upon yourself," he muttered, his voice raw. "She was a threat. She had to be."

But even as he said the words, he felt their hollowness. Mariamne had not been a threat—not to his throne, not to his life. The only thing she had threatened was the fragile veneer of control he clung to so desperately. Her defiance, her strength, had been a mirror that reflected his own weaknesses, and he had destroyed her for it.

The days that followed were a blur of routine and ritual, each one a pale imitation of the life Herod had once known. The court moved cautiously around him, their deference tinged with fear. They whispered of his erratic behavior, of the nights he spent pacing the halls or locking himself away in his chamber. Even Nicolas of Damascus, his most trusted advisor, struggled to reach him.

One evening, as the sun dipped below the horizon, Herod found himself in the gardens where he and Mariamne had once walked. The jasmine blossoms were in full bloom, their scent heavy in the warm night air. He wandered among the flowers, his hands trailing over the delicate petals, until he reached the fountain.

The water was still, its surface reflecting the stars above. Herod knelt beside it, his reflection staring back at him. He barely recognized the man he saw: hollow-eyed, his face lined with grief and regret. He clenched his fists, the cool stone of the fountain biting into his palms.

"What have I become?" he whispered, his voice breaking.

The water offered no answer, only the silent mockery of his reflection.

Herod's descent into madness was slow but relentless. The memory of Mariamne consumed him, invading his thoughts and dreams until he could no longer distinguish between past and present. He saw her in the shadows of the palace, in the faces of the courtiers, in the soft rustle of the wind through the curtains. Her voice echoed in his mind, a haunting melody that would not be silenced.

One night, he woke with a start, his heart pounding. He was certain he had heard her laughter, light and musical, as if she were standing beside him. He rose from his bed, his steps unsteady as he searched the room. But there was nothing, only the emptiness that had become his constant companion.

He sank to the floor, his hands clutching his head. "Forgive me," he murmured, his voice trembling. "Forgive me, Mariamne."

But forgiveness, like peace, was a luxury that eluded him. And as the night stretched on, Herod sat alone in the darkness, a king whose kingdom now seemed as hollow as his soul.

CHAPTER 13: THE SONS' RIVALRY

The opulence of Herod's court concealed an atmosphere of mounting tension. Gold-trimmed columns gleamed in the sunlight that filtered through the intricate latticework, casting fractured shadows across the marble floors. But no amount of grandeur could dispel the shadows that loomed over Herod's family. The weight of betrayal—real or imagined—pressed down on him, and nowhere was that tension more palpable than among his sons.

Antipater, Herod's eldest son from his first marriage, moved through the court like a serpent, his every word dripping in a charm and cunning way. He had mastered the art of feigned loyalty, positioning himself as his father's confidant while undermining his rivals at every turn. His younger half-brothers, Alexander and Aristobulus, the sons of Mariamne, bore the weight of their mother's legacy—a legacy Antipater viewed as a threat to his claim to the throne.

"Father," Antipater said one morning as he joined Herod in the palace gardens. His tone was warm, but his eyes were calculating. "I must speak to you about Alexander and Aristobulus. Their ambitions grow unchecked, and I fear they conspire against you."

Herod, seated on a stone bench beneath a sprawling olive tree, regarded his son with narrowed eyes. The mention of conspiracy struck a chord of paranoia that had only deepened in the wake of Mariamne's execution.

"What proof do you have?" Herod asked, his voice sharp.

Antipater's expression was carefully measured, a mask of concern. "I overheard them speaking in hushed tones late at night. They spoke of alliances, of seizing power. They believe their lineage gives them the right to rule. It pains me to bring this to you, but my loyalty is to you and the kingdom."

Herod's hands clenched into fists, the veins in his neck taut. He had always been wary of the influence Mariamne's sons wielded, their Hasmonean blood a constant reminder of his own precarious legitimacy. Yet, a part of him recoiled at the thought of their treachery.

"Leave me," Herod said abruptly, his voice tinged with both anger and uncertainty. "I will consider what you have said."

Antipater bowed, a glimmer of satisfaction in his eyes as he retreated. The seeds of doubt had been planted, and he knew they would take root.

Alexander and Aristobulus were unaware of the storm brewing against them. They moved through the palace with confidence born of youth and privilege, their bond unshaken by the machinations of the court. Yet, beneath their camaraderie lay an undercurrent of frustration, a shared resentment toward their father for the execution of their mother.

"Do you ever wonder if he regrets it?" Aristobulus asked one evening as they sparred in the courtyard, their wooden practice swords clashing with sharp cracks.

Alexander hesitated, lowering his sword. "Regret? I doubt he even feels it. He sees betrayal in every shadow, even where there is none. That paranoia will destroy him—and us, if we are not careful."

Aristobulus frowned, his grip tightening on his sword. "We

cannot let it. We must remain united, no matter what he throws at us."

Alexander nodded, but unease flickered in his eyes. He knew the dangers they faced, but he also knew how easily unity could crumble under the weight of suspicion.

Herod's paranoia festered in the days that followed. Antipater's words replayed in his mind, each repetition adding fuel to his fears. He began to scrutinize Alexander and Aristobulus more closely, searching for signs of rebellion. Their laughter, once a source of pride, now sounded like mockery. Their confidence felt like defiance.

One evening, during a lavish banquet, Herod's suspicions reached a boiling point. The hall was filled with the clatter of silverware and the murmur of conversation, but Herod's focus was fixed on his sons. Alexander and Aristobulus sat together, their heads bowed in quiet conversation. To Herod, their gestures seemed conspiratorial, their glances pointed.

Unable to contain himself, Herod slammed his goblet onto the table, the sound silencing the room. "What treachery do you whisper about now?" he demanded, his voice echoing off the gilded walls.

Alexander and Aristobulus exchanged startled looks before Alexander spoke, his tone measured. "Father, we speak of nothing but mundane matters. Why do you accuse us so freely?"

Herod rose from his seat, his eyes blazing. "Do not play innocent with me. I know of your ambitions, your plots. You would see me dead if it meant seizing my throne."

Aristobulus stood, his youthful pride flaring. "We are your sons! How can you believe such lies? We have done nothing but serve you faithfully."

Herod's lips curled into a snarl. "Your mother's blood runs through your veins. Her defiance, her treachery—it lives in you. Guards! Take them to the dungeons."

The court erupted into shocked murmurs as soldiers stepped forward, their hands hesitating as they seized the princes. Alexander and Aristobulus struggled, their protests echoing through the hall, but Herod turned away, his heart a storm of anger and anguish.

The dungeons were cold and damp, the air thick with the scent of mildew. Alexander and Aristobulus sat on the stone floor, their faces pale but resolute. They had been stripped of their finery, their chains a cruel reminder of their father's distrust.

"This is Antipater's doing," Aristobulus said bitterly, his voice a low growl. "He's poisoned Father against us."

Alexander nodded; his jaw clenched. "We must find a way to prove our innocence. Father's mind is clouded, but perhaps... perhaps we can reach him."

Aristobulus shook his head. "You still believe he can be reasoned with? He sees us as enemies, Alexander. He's too far gone."

Their conversation was interrupted by the sound of footsteps echoing through the corridor. A guard appeared; his expression grim.

"The king has summoned you," he said.

The brothers exchanged a wary glance before rising, their chains clinking as they followed the guard. Whatever awaited them, they would face it together.

Herod sat on his throne, his face, a mask of stone as Alexander and Aristobulus were brought before him. The court was silent, the tension palpable. Antipater stood to the side, his expression carefully neutral, though a glimmer of triumph shone in his eyes.

"You stand accused of plotting against your king," Herod said, his voice cold. "Have you anything to say in your defense?"

Alexander stepped forward, his chains rattling. "Father, we are your sons. We have served you loyally, despite the pain you have caused us. These accusations are false, born of envy and deceit. Do not let Antipater's lies poison your judgment."

Herod's gaze flickered, but he quickly hardened his expression. "Antipater has brought me evidence, witnesses. What do you offer but words?"

Aristobulus's temper flared. "Words are all we have because the truth needs no embellishment. Antipater has manipulated you, Father, and you are too blind to see it."

Herod rose, his voice a thunderclap. "Enough! I will not be lectured by my own sons. Guards, take them away. Their fate is sealed."

The court erupted into chaos as Alexander and Aristobulus were dragged from the hall, their protests ringing in Herod's ears. He returned to his throne, his hands trembling as he gripped the armrests. Antipater approached, his voice low and soothing.

"You did what was necessary, Father," he said. "For the good of the kingdom."

Herod said nothing, his thoughts a maelstrom of doubt and regret.

The execution of Alexander and Aristobulus marked a turning point in Herod's reign. The people mourned the loss of the young princes, their grief mingling with anger. The court grew colder, its members treading carefully around a king whose paranoia had reached dangerous heights.

Herod, for all his outward resolve, was haunted by his actions. He saw Alexander's steady gaze, Aristobulus's fiery defiance, in his dreams. Their voices echoed in his mind, accusing and unrelenting.

And as he wandered the empty halls of his palace, Herod realized that he had destroyed not only his sons but also the last remnants of the family he had once fought to build.

CHAPTER 14: CAESAREA MARITIMA

The coastline of Judea stretched out like a glittering promise beneath the midday sun. Waves lapped gently at the shore, their rhythm broken only by the sounds of construction: the hammering of chisels on stone, the creak of pulleys lifting massive blocks, and the shouted commands of overseers driving their workers to the brink of exhaustion. Above it all stood Herod, his figure silhouetted against the azure sky as he surveyed his grand creation.

Caesarea Maritima was more than a city; it was a statement, a monument to Herod's ambition and his desire to leave a legacy that would endure for centuries. The port was unlike anything Judea had ever seen. Its harbor, built with innovative hydraulic concrete that hardened underwater, extended into the sea like a hand reaching for the world. The streets were wide and orderly, lined with colonnades and adorned with statues imported from Greece and Rome. At its heart stood a massive temple dedicated to Augustus, its white marble gleaming like a beacon of Herod's loyalty to the empire.

Herod turned to Nicolas of Damascus, who stood at his side. "Look at it, Nicolas," he said, his voice filled with a rare note of pride. "A city that rivals anything in the empire. Here, Judea will trade with the world. Here, my name will be remembered."

Nicolas nodded, his expression thoughtful. "It is a marvel, my king. But the people... they wonder if it was worth the cost."

Herod's smile faltered, his gaze hardening. "The people do not understand greatness. They see only the burden of the present, not the glory of the future. History will vindicate me."

For the workers who had built Caesarea, the city was less a marvel and more a testament to their suffering. Yoram, now a foreman, watched as the final touches were put on the harbor's breakwaters. His hands, once roughened by years of chiseling stone, now bore the scars of overseeing countless laborers. Around him, men toiled under the relentless sun, their faces etched with exhaustion and resentment.

"They'll praise the king," one worker muttered, his voice laced with bitterness. "But they'll forget us. The ones who bled for this."

Yoram placed a hand on the man's shoulder. "They may forget our names, but they won't forget our work. This city will stand long after we are gone."

The worker snorted. "Easy to say when you're not breaking your back to lift these stones."

Yoram said nothing, his gaze drifting to the harbor. He had risen through the ranks not by choice but by necessity, his loyalty to the workers clashing with his need to survive in a kingdom that demanded absolute obedience. He understood their anger, but he also knew the futility of open defiance. Herod's reach was long, and his wrath unforgiving.

The day of the city's unveiling dawned with a brilliance that seemed almost orchestrated. The sky was cloudless, the sea a shimmering expanse of blue. Delegates from across the empire gathered in Caesarea's grand amphitheater, their garments resplendent with the colors of their regions. The air buzzed with anticipation as Herod stepped onto the stage, his robes of crimson and gold catching the sunlight.

He raised his hands, and the crowd fell silent.

"Citizens of Judea and honored guests," Herod began, his voice resonant and commanding. "Behold Caesarea Maritima, a city born of vision and perseverance. This harbor will connect Judea to the farthest corners of the empire, bringing prosperity and unity. This temple, dedicated to Augustus, stands as a testament to our loyalty and our place within Rome's great dominion."

The crowd erupted into applause, the sound echoing through the amphitheater. Herod's chest swelled with pride as he basked in their adulation. Yet, even as he smiled, a shadow lingered in his mind. He could feel the undercurrent of dissent, the invisible threads of discontent that threatened to unravel his carefully constructed world.

As the festivities continued, Yoram watched from the shadows, his expression unreadable. The workers had been allowed to attend the celebration, their presence a token acknowledgment of their labor. But they stood apart, their worn clothing and tired faces a stark contrast to the opulence of the visiting dignitaries.

"Do you think he even sees us?" the same worker from before asked, his voice low.

Yoram's eyes remained fixed on Herod. "He sees us. But only as tools. Tools to build his dreams."

The worker shook his head. "Dreams built on our bones. That's what they'll remember."

That evening, as the city's new streets were lit by the flickering glow of torches, Herod retired to his private chamber overlooking the harbor. The view was breathtaking, the moonlight dancing on the water, the sounds of celebration drifting up from the city below. But Herod's mind was restless.

Nicolas entered; his expression thoughtful. "The unveiling was a success, my king. The delegates were impressed, and the people... well, they are awed by your achievement."

Herod turned to him; his eyes shadowed. “And yet, I sense their resentment. They cheer for me today, but tomorrow they will curse my name. They see only the cost, not the vision.”

Nicolas hesitated. “Vision requires sacrifice, my king. But sacrifice breeds discontent. It is a delicate balance.”

Herod’s gaze returned to the harbor. “Balance. A word that sounds so simple, yet it eludes me. I have built cities, temples, and fortresses. I have crushed rebellions and secured alliances. And still, it is never enough.”

“Perhaps,” Nicolas ventured carefully, “it is not about what you build, but what you leave behind.”

Herod’s lips twisted into a bitter smile. “What I leave behind will be judged by history. And history is written by those who survive.”

In the weeks that followed, Caesarea Maritima became a bustling hub of activity. Traders and merchants flocked to its harbor, their ships carrying goods from every corner of the empire. The city thrived, its streets alive with the sounds of commerce and culture. But beneath the surface, the exploitation that had built it remained a raw wound.

Yoram continued his work, overseeing repairs and expansions as the city grew. But the resentment among the workers festered, their anger simmering just below the surface. For every statue erected, for every street paved, they saw the toll it had taken on their bodies and their spirits.

One evening, as Yoram walked along the harbor, he paused to watch the sunset. The water glowed with hues of orange and gold; a sight so beautiful it almost eased the ache in his chest. Almost.

“Do you think it was worth it?” a voice asked behind him.

Yoram turned to see the worker who had spoken to him so often, his expression weary but determined.

“Worth it?” Yoram repeated, his voice was heavy. “For Herod, perhaps. For us? I don’t know.”

The worker nodded; his gaze fixed on the horizon. "Maybe one day, someone will remember. Not just the king, but the ones who built his dreams."

Yoram said nothing, his thoughts as restless as the waves at his feet. And as the sun dipped below the horizon, he wondered if the grandeur of Caesarea would ever be enough to justify the cost.

CHAPTER 15: THE BETHLEHEM RUMORS

The palace was still, its marble halls cloaked in an uneasy quiet. Herod stood by the window of his private chamber; his gaze fixed on the distant hills that surrounded Jerusalem. The faint light of dawn crept over the horizon, casting the landscape in muted gold. Yet, the beauty of the scene did little to ease the storm brewing within him. A whisper of prophecy had reached his ears, a murmur carried on the winds of the restless countryside.

A child, born to be "King of the Jews."

The words gnawed at Herod's thoughts; their simplicity belied by the threat they carried. He had spent his life consolidating power, crushing rebellion, and silencing dissent, all to secure his throne. Yet now, a nameless child threatened to undo it all.

Nicolas of Damascus entered the room, his expression grave. "My king, the rumors grow. The Magi from the East claim to have seen a star heralding the birth of this child. They speak of him as a king chosen by divine will."

Herod turned, his eyes dark and searching. "A child," he said, his voice low and sharp. "A child who would dare challenge my reign. Do they think me so weak, so easily replaced?"

Nicolas hesitated. "Prophecies are dangerous, my king, not

because of their truth, but because of the faith they inspire. The people are desperate for hope, and such whispers can ignite a fire we may not be able to control."

Herod's jaw tightened. "Hope is a weapon more dangerous than any sword. Find this child, Nicolas. And ensure he does not live to threaten me."

The search began with quiet efficiency. Spies were dispatched to Bethlehem and the surrounding regions, their task to uncover any clue that might lead to the child. The Magi were summoned to the palace, their mysterious air both intriguing and infuriating to Herod. They spoke in riddles, their reverence for the prophecy palpable.

"We seek the one who is born King of the Jews," one of them said, his tone measured but firm. "The star has guided us this far, and we believe he lies in Bethlehem."

Herod's smile was a mask, his voice smooth. "Go, then. Find this child and bring me word, so that I too may honor him."

But as the Magi departed, Herod's mask slipped, his true intentions simmering beneath the surface. He could not afford to wait for their return. The threat had to be eliminated at its root.

The soldiers came at night, their armor glinting in the pale light of the moon. They moved through the narrow streets of Bethlehem with grim determination, their orders clear and unyielding. Doors were forced open, cries of alarm echoing through the quiet town as mothers clutched their children and fathers pleaded for mercy.

In one small house at the edge of the town, a young couple huddled in fear. Miriam held her infant son tightly against her chest, her breath shallow as she listened to the approaching footsteps. Her husband, Eli, peered through the cracks of the door, his face pale.

"They're coming," he whispered, his voice trembling. "We have to go."

Miriam shook her head, tears streaming down her face. "There's nowhere to go. They'll find us."

Eli knelt beside her; his hands steady despite his fear. "Listen to me. We can't stay here. The hills—we can hide there until they're gone."

With trembling hands, Miriam wrapped her son in a thin blanket, muffling his cries as they slipped out the back of the house. The streets were chaos, filled with the sounds of wailing and the clash of steel. They moved quickly, keeping to the shadows, their hearts pounding with every step.

From his balcony, Herod watched the distant hills, his expression unreadable. The reports would come soon, confirmation that the threat had been neutralized. Yet, even as he stood in the stillness of the night, a part of him wavered. He thought of his own children, their laughter echoing through the halls, their small hands reaching for him.

But this was different, he told himself. This was survival. A single child's life was a small price to pay for the security of a kingdom.

Miriam and Eli reached the edge of the town just as the soldiers arrived at their home. They hid among the rocks, their breaths shallow as they watched the flames rise in the distance. Miriam clutched her son tightly, her tears soaking into the fabric of his blanket.

"Will they stop?" she whispered, her voice barely audible.

Eli shook his head. "Not until they've done what they came to do."

The night stretched on, the cries of the town mingling with the crackle of fire. Miriam closed her eyes, her heart breaking for those left behind. She thought of her neighbors, her friends, and their children. And she prayed—for mercy, for justice, for a future where such horrors would not be repeated.

When the soldiers returned to Jerusalem, their report was brief and brutal. The task was complete, the threat eliminated. Herod listened in silence; his expression unreadable. But as the soldiers left, heaviness settled over him, a weight that no amount of justification could lift.

He returned to his chamber, the walls closing in around him. The whispers of prophecy still lingered in his mind, now mingled with the cries of the innocent. He had silenced one threat, but in doing so, he had planted the seeds of another—a legacy of fear and cruelty that would haunt him for the rest of his days.

And as the city slept, Herod sat alone in the darkness, a king whose throne was built on the fragile foundation of paranoia and bloodshed.

CHAPTER 16: THE BUILDER'S CURSE

The desert stretched endlessly, its ochre sands shimmering under the searing sun. Masada, Herod's latest masterpiece, rose defiantly from the barren landscape, a fortress carved from the sheer cliffs as if to challenge the heavens themselves. From its walls, the view extended to the Dead Sea, a glistening expanse of saltwater that mirrored the harsh beauty of the Judean wilderness. To Herod, Masada was not just a stronghold; it was a sanctuary, a testament to his power, and a shield against the enemies he was certain lurked in every shadow.

Standing on the ramparts, Herod surveyed the construction below. Hundreds of laborers moved like ants, hauling stones and mixing mortar under the watchful eyes of overseers. The sounds of their labor—the rhythmic pounding of hammers, the scrape of chisels, and the occasional shouted command—rose in a cacophony that echoed off the cliffs.

Nicolas of Damascus stood at Herod's side; his expression pensive. "Masada will endure, my king," he said. "Its walls are impenetrable, its storehouses plentiful. It is a fortress worthy of legend."

Herod nodded; his gaze fixed on the workers below. "It must endure," he said, his voice low and resolute. "For when the world turns against me—and it will—Masada will be my refuge."

Nicolas hesitated. "Do you believe that time will come?"

Herod turned to him, his eyes dark and unreadable. "Paranoia is a word used by those who lack enemies. I have enemies, Nicolas. They are everywhere. Masada is my answer to their schemes."

For the laborers, Masada was a testament not to power but to suffering. The heat was relentless, the work grueling, and the conditions unforgiving. Yoram, now an experienced foreman, moved among the workers, his presence both a comfort and a reminder of the harsh realities they faced.

"Keep the lines tight," he called out as a group of men hoisted a massive stone block into place. Sweat dripped from their brows, their muscles straining under the weight.

One of the workers stumbled, his grip faltering. The block swayed precariously, eliciting shouts of alarm. Yoram rushed forward, his hands steadying the rope. "Hold it! Steady now!"

The crisis passed, but the tension lingered. Yoram's gaze swept over the men, their faces etched with exhaustion. He knew the toll this project was taking, but there was little he could do. To question the king's ambition was to invite ruin.

As the weeks turned to months, Masada neared completion. The palace, perched at the northern tip of the plateau, was a marvel of engineering. Its terraced levels cascaded down the cliffside, each tier adorned with columns, frescoes, and mosaic floors that rivaled those of Rome. Cisterns carved deep into the rock held enough water to sustain a siege, while granaries brimmed with provisions.

Herod walked through the halls of the palace, his footsteps echoing in the vast, empty spaces. He ran his hand along the cool stone walls, marveling at their strength. This was his sanctuary, his fortress against the world. And yet, as he stood alone in its grandeur, a flicker of doubt crept into his mind.

He thought of Mariamne, of Alexander and Aristobulus, of the countless lives he had sacrificed to secure his throne. Masada was a monument to his success, but it was also a symbol of his isolation. He had built walls to keep his enemies out, but in doing so, he had trapped himself within.

The accident happened on a clear, cloudless morning. The workers were lowering a massive stone lintel into place, their movements synchronized under Yoram's watchful eye. The block hung suspended from a series of ropes and pulleys, its weight was a testament to the ingenuity of Herod's engineers.

A sharp crack split the air, followed by shouts of alarm. One of the ropes had snapped, its fibers worn thin from months of use. The block lurched to one side, the remaining ropes straining under the sudden shift in weight.

"Get clear!" Yoram shouted, his voice cutting through the chaos. But it was too late. The block plummeted, striking the scaffolding below with a deafening crash. Wooden beams splintered, and workers were thrown from their perches, their cries of terror mingling with the groan of collapsing structures.

When the dust settled, the scene was one of devastation. Bodies lay scattered among the rubble, their forms twisted and broken. Survivors moved among them, their faces pale with shock as they searched for the living and the dead.

Herod arrived moments later; his expression grim. He surveyed the destruction, his gaze lingering on the lifeless forms of the workers. For a moment, he said nothing, the weight of the scene pressing down on him.

"How many?" he asked finally, his voice quiet.

Yoram stepped forward, his face lined with grief. "At least twenty, my king. Perhaps more."

Herod's jaw tightened. "Ensure the dead are buried with dignity. Their families will be compensated."

Yoram nodded, though he knew the compensation would do little to ease the pain of loss. "And the work, my king?"

Herod's gaze shifted to the unfinished palace, its walls still incomplete. "The work continues. Masada must be finished."

The accident cast a shadow over the final days of construction. The workers moved with a quiet solemnity, their usual banter replaced by a heavy silence. Yoram did his best to keep morale high, but he could see the toll the project was taking. Every stone lifted, every wall erected, was a reminder of the price they had paid.

Herod, too, felt the weight of the tragedy. He spent his nights wandering the halls of the nearly completed palace, his thoughts a tumult of ambition and regret. Masada was his refuge, but it was also a monument to his paranoia, a fortress built on the backs of those who had no choice but to obey.

When Masada was finally complete, Herod stood on the highest terrace, gazing out over the desert. The fortress was everything he had envisioned: impregnable, self-sustaining, a symbol of his power. Yet, as the wind whipped through the cliffs, he felt no triumph, only a hollow ache.

Nicolas joined him, his expression reflective. "Masada is a masterpiece, my king. It will stand for centuries."

Herod nodded, though his gaze remained fixed on the horizon. "It will stand," he said. "But at what cost?"

Nicolas hesitated, then placed a hand on Herod's shoulder. "The cost is for history to judge. For now, you have built something that will outlast us all."

Herod said nothing, his thoughts a labyrinth of doubt and determination. Masada was his greatest achievement, but it was also a reminder of all he had lost. And as he stood on its walls, the wind carrying the echoes of the workers' labor, he wondered if the fortress was truly a sanctuary or merely another prison.

CHAPTER 17: THE FALL OF ANTIPATER

The corridors of Herod's palace, once bustling with activity, now seemed to echo with an oppressive silence. The light streaming through the high windows cast long shadows across the polished floors, lending an eerie stillness to the air. Herod sat alone in his chamber, the weight of his crown pressing down on him like a physical burden. His once-unwavering confidence had eroded, leaving in its place a cauldron of doubt and regret.

The betrayal that had haunted his life was no longer a phantom whisper in the night. It had taken shape, emerging not from distant enemies or shadowy conspiracies but from his own blood. Antipater, the son he had once entrusted with the future of his kingdom, was plotting against him.

Nicolas of Damascus entered cautiously, a scroll in his hand. His expression was grave, his usual calm demeanor shaken by the gravity of what he carried.

"My king," Nicolas said, bowing deeply. "The evidence is undeniable. Antipater has conspired with Rome's envoys and certain members of your court. His ambition knows no bounds."

Herod took the scroll, his hands trembling slightly as he unrolled it. The words before him detailed a web of deceit that made his stomach churn. Antipater had forged alliances, spread falsehoods, and even attempted to poison him. Herod's vision blurred as he read, each line a dagger to his already wounded heart.

"Bring him to me," Herod said finally, his voice a low growl.

Nicolas hesitated. "My king, perhaps... it would be wise to consider your approach. Antipater is cunning. He may attempt to sway your judgment."

Herod's gaze snapped to Nicolas, his eyes blazing. "Do you think me so weak, Nicolas? Bring him."

Antipater entered the chamber with his usual air of confidence, his robes impeccably arranged, his expression one of feigned concern. He knelt before Herod, his movements deliberate, his voice smooth.

"Father, you summoned me. How may I serve you?"

Herod's lips curled into a bitter smile. "Serve me, Antipater? Tell me, how does one serve a father while plotting his demise?"

Antipater's face betrayed a flicker of surprise before he masked it with indignation. "My king, I know not what you mean. I have always been loyal to you, to our family, to Judea."

Herod rose from his seat, towering over his son. He held the scroll aloft, his hand shaking with fury. "Lies and poison, Antipater! That is your loyalty. I trusted you above all others, and this is how you repay me?"

Antipater's composure began to crack. He fell to his knees, his voice pleading. "Father, these accusations are false! Someone seeks to turn you against me. You know how the court envies my position, how they spread rumors to destroy me."

Herod's hand lashed out, striking Antipater across the face. The sound echoed through the chamber, followed by a heavy silence.

"Do not take me for a fool," Herod said, his voice deadly calm. "I have seen the letters, heard the testimonies. Your ambition has blinded you, Antipater, and now you will face the consequences."

Antipater's defiance flared, his voice rising. "And what of your ambition, Father? You have destroyed everyone who stood in your way. Your wives, your sons, your allies. You rule a kingdom of ashes, and you dare to judge me?"

Herod's expression darkened, the truth of Antipater's words cutting deeper than any blade. He turned away, his back to his son, as he struggled to compose himself.

"Guards," Herod said finally, his voice heavy with resolve. "Take him to the dungeons. He will stand trial for his treason."

The trial of Antipater was a spectacle unlike any the court had seen. The chamber was filled with courtiers, advisors, and envoys, all eager to witness the fall of the favored son. The evidence against him was overwhelming: letters intercepted by Herod's spies, testimonies from those he had conspired with, even poison found hidden among his belongings.

Antipater stood before the court; his once-proud demeanor reduced to desperation. He denied the charges with fervor, accusing his accusers of jealousy and deceit. But his words carried little weight against the mountain of proof presented by Herod's prosecutors.

Herod watched in silence, his expression a mask of stoicism. But inside, his heart ached. This was his son, the boy he had once held in his arms, the heir he had groomed to carry on his legacy. Yet now, that legacy was crumbling, a reflection of the betrayal and ambition that had defined his reign.

When the verdict was announced, a murmur rippled through the court. Antipater was found guilty of treason and sentenced to death. Herod's hand trembled as he signed the order, the weight of the decision pressing down on him like a physical burden.

The execution took place at dawn. The air was cool, the sky painted with hues of pink and gold as the first light of day crept over the horizon. Antipater stood on the platform, his face pale but composed. He glanced at the gathered crowd, his gaze lingering on Herod, who watched from the palace balcony.

"Father," Antipater called out, his voice carrying over the hushed assembly. "Remember this day, for it is the day you destroyed your own blood. You may claim victory, but your throne is built on sand. It will not hold."

Herod said nothing, his expression unreadable. He watched as the executioner stepped forward, his sword gleaming in the morning light. The blade fell swiftly, and with it, the last vestiges of Herod's family.

The days that followed were marked by a suffocating silence. Herod retreated to his chambers, shunning the court and its intrigues. He wandered the halls of the palace, his thoughts a labyrinth of regret and reflection. The faces of those he had lost haunted him: Mariamne, Alexander, Aristobulus, and now Antipater.

He stood in front of a mirror, his reflection staring back at him with hollow eyes. The man who had conquered kingdoms, built cities, and secured a legacy now seemed a shadow of himself. His crown, once a symbol of triumph, now felt like a shackle.

Nicolas of Damascus found him there, with concern. "My king," he said gently, "you cannot undo what has been done. But you can still shape what remains. Judea needs its king."

Herod's gaze shifted to Nicolas, his voice a whisper. "A king? Or a butcher? Tell me, Nicolas, how will history remember me?"

Nicolas hesitated, choosing his words carefully. "History will remember a man who built greatness from chaos, who secured his kingdom against all odds. But it will also remember the cost. Only you can decide which legacy will endure."

Herod turned away, his reflection disappearing into the shadows. The weight of his choices pressed down on him, a burden he would carry until his dying breath. And as the sun set over Jerusalem, the king who had ruled with an iron fist found himself alone, the echoes of his ambition reverberating through the empty halls.

CHAPTER 18: ILLNESS AND ISOLATION

The once-mighty palace of Herod had grown quiet, its gilded halls now haunted by an oppressive stillness. The king, who had ruled with such ruthless ambition, was confined to his chamber. Outside, the world continued, but within these walls, time seemed to stand still, as though the very air held its breath in anticipation of what was to come.

Herod lay in his grand bed, a shadow of his former self. His body, once robust and commanding, was now gaunt and frail. The relentless pain that coursed through him left him trembling, his breath ragged. His attendants moved like wraiths, their faces etched with worry as they tended to him with a mixture of duty and fear. The stench of sickness clung to the air, a sour reminder of the inevitability that even kings could not escape.

"Leave me," Herod rasped, his voice barely above a whisper.

The attendants hesitated but obeyed, bowing as they exited. The door creaked shut behind them, leaving Herod alone with his thoughts. Or so he thought.

A soft, familiar voice broke the silence. "Herod."

His eyes snapped open, his heart pounding. He turned his head, searching for the dimly lit room. There, in the shadows, stood Mariamne, her form as vivid as the day he had last seen her. She was dressed in white, her hair cascading over her shoulders, her gaze piercing.

“You,” Herod whispered, his voice trembling. “How can this be?”

Mariamne stepped closer; her movements graceful, almost ethereal. “Did you think you could silence me forever?” she said, her tone tinged with sorrow. “I live in your mind, Herod. In your regrets, your fears. You cannot escape me.”

Herod squeezed his eyes shut, shaking his head as if to dispel the vision. “You are not real. This is... a trick of my mind.”

“And yet,” she replied, her voice softening, “I am here. Tell me, Herod, was it worth it? Your crown, your fortresses, your power? Was it worth the lives you took, the love you destroyed?”

The hallucinations came and went with cruel unpredictability. Sometimes it was Mariamne, her presence, a reminder of the love he had squandered. Other times, it was Alexander and Aristobulus, their youthful faces twisted with accusations. They appeared in the corners of his vision, their voices echoing in his mind, dragging him deeper into his torment.

“Father,” Alexander’s voice whispered one night as Herod lay in a fevered state. “You killed us for fear of losing your throne. And now, what do you rule? Shadows and emptiness.”

Herod’s hands clawed at the sheets, his chest heaving. “I did what I had to,” he muttered. “To protect the kingdom.”

“A kingdom built on blood,” Aristobulus’s voice replied. “And blood will be its undoing.”

The nights were the worst, the darkness amplifying his fears and regrets. But in the rare moments of clarity, Herod’s mind drifted to his childhood. He saw his mother, Cypros, her stern face framed by the dim light of their modest home. She had been a woman of sharp intellect and unyielding resolve, her words often harsh but always meant to prepare him for the life she knew awaited.

“The world is full of betrayal, Herod,” she had told him once, her voice steady as she brushed a hand through his hair. "Even those closest to you will turn against you if given the chance. Trust no one. Protect what is yours at all costs."

As a boy, Herod had absorbed her warnings like scripture. He had seen her words play out in the treacheries of court life, in the ambitions of his rivals. But now, as he lay on the precipice of death, he wondered if her teachings had not shielded him but condemned him. Trust no one. Protect what is yours. Those mantras had guided his life, but they had also left him alone.

Nicolas of Damascus visited frequently, though Herod's lucidity waned with each passing day. The advisor sat by his bedside one evening, the room dimly lit by a single lamp. Herod's eyes fluttered open, and for a moment, recognition flickered in their depths.

"Nicolas," he murmured. "You... you have always been loyal."

Nicolas inclined his head. "I have served you to the best of my ability, my king."

Herod's lips twitched in what might have been a smile. "Tell me... do you think they will remember me? Truly remember me?"

Nicolas hesitated, choosing his words carefully. "History will remember your achievements, my king. Your cities, your fortresses, your vision. But it will also remember the cost."

Herod's expression darkened, his gaze drifting to the ceiling. "The cost," he repeated. "Always the cost. Was there any other way?"

Nicolas leaned forward, his voice gentle. "Perhaps, my king. But the path you chose was the one you believed necessary. And that is the burden of kings."

The days blended together, each one marked by the slow unraveling of Herod's body and mind. The fever that consumed him brought new visions, more vivid and unrelenting. He saw Mariamne's eyes, filled with a mix of love and betrayal. He heard Alexander and Aristobulus laughing, their voices tinged with bitterness. Even Antipater appeared, his expression was one of defiance and triumph.

"You were wrong about me, Father," Antipater's voice sneered. "But then, you were wrong about many things."

Herod screamed, the sound raw and broken. The attendants rushed in, their faces pale with fear as they tried to calm him. But nothing could quiet the ghosts that haunted him.

One night, as the moon cast its pale light over the palace, Herod found a moment of clarity. He sat upright in his bed, his breathing labored but steady. He called for Nicolas, who arrived promptly, his expression was one of quiet concern.

"Nicolas," Herod said, his voice weak but firm. "I want you to write something for me. A testament. Not to the world, but to those who will come after me."

Nicolas nodded, retrieving a scroll and quill. "I am ready, my king."

Herod closed his eyes, gathering his thoughts. "Write this: 'To rule is to sacrifice. To build is to destroy. I have done both, and I will bear the weight of those choices for eternity. May those who follow find a better way.'"

Nicolas wrote in silence, the quill scratching softly against the parchment. When he finished, he looked up to find Herod staring at him, his gaze piercing despite his frailty.

"Do you believe they will?" Herod asked, his voice barely above a whisper.

Nicolas hesitated, then nodded. "I believe they will try, my king."

Herod sank back into his pillows, his eyes closing. The room fell silent once more, save for the faint rustle of the wind through the curtains. And as the king drifted into a restless sleep, his dreams filled with the faces of those he had loved and lost, the palace seemed to hold its breath, waiting for the end.

CHAPTER 19: A KINGDOM DIVIDED

The golden glow of the setting sunbathed the palace in an ethereal light, casting long shadows across its marble halls. Herod sat at the center of his chamber; a thick scroll of parchment unfurled before him. His hands trembled as he gripped the quill, each stroke of ink a painful reminder of the legacy he was about to leave behind. The weight of the moment pressed down on him, more suffocating than the illness ravaging his body.

Rome had already begun its quiet encroachment. The representatives sent by Augustus loitered in the palace, their presence a silent reminder that Judea's fate was no longer entirely Herod's to decide. Yet, even now, Herod clung to the illusion of control, drafting his will with the meticulousness that had defined his rule.

"Divide the kingdom," he muttered, his voice hoarse and uneven. "It is the only way."

Nicolas of Damascus, seated across from him, regarded the king with a mixture of loyalty and apprehension. The scroll he held listed the names of Herod's surviving sons: Archelaus, Antipas, and Philip. Each name carried the weight of potential but also the shadow of doubt. Herod's family had been fractured by betrayal and ambition; now, his final act would either heal those fractures or deepen them.

"Are you certain, my king?" Nicolas asked cautiously. "Dividing the kingdom may prevent immediate conflict, but it could sow seeds of discord for the future."

Herod's gaze sharpened, his eyes glinting with the fire of his former self. "I have no illusions about my sons, Nicolas. Each of them carries ambition in their veins. But united, they will destroy one another. Divided, they may yet survive."

The first draft of the will designated Archelaus as ruler of Judea and Samaria, the heart of Herod's kingdom. Antipas was to govern Galilee and Perea, regions rich in culture and trade. Philip would inherit the territories to the east of the Jordan, lands less fertile but strategically vital. Each inheritance reflected Herod's calculations, his attempts to balance power and mitigate conflict.

But even as the divisions were finalized, the specter of Rome loomed large. Herod's kingdom would not pass seamlessly into his sons' hands. The Roman representatives, with their polished diplomacy and veiled threats, ensured that Judea's future remained under the watchful eye of the empire.

At the banquet that evening, Herod summoned his sons to the great hall. The room, once a place of celebration and grandeur, now felt heavy with unspoken tension. Archelaus, tall and imposing, sat at one end of the table, his expression a mask of stoic confidence. Antipas, smaller but no less shrewd, leaned back in his chair, his sharp eyes scanning the room. Philip, quieter and more introspective, sat apart, his gaze focused on the goblet of wine in his hands.

Herod entered, supported by attendants, his presence still commanding despite his frailty. The murmurs ceased as he approached the head of the table, his sons rising in deference.

"Sit," Herod said, his voice steady but devoid of warmth. "We have much to discuss."

As they obeyed, he surveyed them with a critical eye, searching for signs of dissent. "You are my sons, the heirs to my kingdom. But you are also men, each with your own ambitions, your own desires. What I give you tonight is both a gift and a burden."

He gestured to Nicolas, who unfurled the will. The sound of parchment unfurling was deafening in the silence.

"Archelaus," Herod began, his gaze fixed on his eldest. "You will rule Judea and Samaria. They are the heart of this kingdom, the seat of its power. But they are also the most volatile. Govern them wisely, or they will consume you."

Archelaus inclined his head, his expression unreadable. "I will honor your trust, Father."

"Antipas," Herod continued, turning to his second son. "Galilee and Perea will be yours. They are prosperous regions, but they demand a ruler who understands their people. Do not underestimate the responsibility you carry."

Antipas smirked faintly, his confidence bordering on arrogance. "You will not be disappointed, Father."

"And Philip," Herod said, his tone softening slightly. "The lands east of the Jordan will be yours. They are not as wealthy, but they are vital to our defenses. Your wisdom will serve you well."

Philip nodded, his voice quiet. "Thank you, Father."

The announcement was met with polite acknowledgments, but beneath the surface, tensions simmered. Archelaus's stoicism concealed a growing resentment toward Antipas, whose confidence grated on him. Philip, though less ambitious, could feel the weight of his brothers' scrutiny, their unspoken judgments cast a shadow over his inheritance.

After the banquet, Herod retreated to his chamber, his body trembling from the exertion. Nicolas joined him, his expression unreadable.

"It is done," Herod said, sinking into his chair. "Now it is up to them."

"Do you believe they will honor your wishes?" Nicolas asked.

Herod's lips twisted into a bitter smile. "They will fight. Of that, I am certain. But Rome will decide their fate in the end. Perhaps that is for the best. A divided kingdom is easier to control."

The Roman envoys, led by Quintus Varro, convened with Nicolas the following day. The men, dressed in the fine togas of imperial officials, carried themselves with an air of detached authority.

"Herod's will is clear," Nicolas explained, presenting the document. "Each son will govern their respective regions, as outlined here."

Varro examined the parchment, his expression neutral. "And what of Rome's interests? Herod's kingdom exists at the pleasure of Augustus. It is not simply his to divide."

Nicolas stiffened but maintained his composure. "The division ensures stability, which serves both Judea and Rome. Herod has always been loyal to the empire. His final wish reflects that loyalty."

Varro's lips twitched in what might have been a smile. "We shall see. The Senate will review the will, and Augustus will make the final determination. Until then, we will observe."

Herod watched from his balcony as the Roman delegation departed, their horses kicking up clouds of dust. The sight filled him with a mixture of relief and despair. He had done everything he could to secure his legacy, but the future was now out of his hands.

That night, as he lay in bed, the faces of his sons haunted him. He saw Archelaus's stoic mask, Antipas's sly grin, and Philip's quiet resolve. He saw flashes of their future—the conflicts, betrayals, the inevitable interference of Rome.

And as sleep claimed him, Herod dreamed of his kingdom, its walls crumbling, its people scattered. In his dream, the throne stood empty, a stark reminder that even the greatest rulers could not escape the ravages of time and ambition.

CHAPTER 20: THE DEATH OF HEROD

The air in Herod's chamber was thick, heavy with the pungent aroma of incense and the faint metallic tang of blood. The once-grand room, adorned with tapestries and gold-leafed columns, felt claustrophobic, its opulence dimmed by the shadows of impending death. Herod lay on a bed draped in fine silks, his body wracked with pain that no physician could soothe. The mighty king who had bent nations to his will was now reduced to a trembling, broken man.

His attendants moved with hushed reverence, their eyes avoiding his. Fear clung to them like a second skin; the king's paranoia had outlived his strength. Even in his final hours, Herod's presence commanded unease, as if the force of his will alone could reach beyond the grave.

"Bring Nicolas," Herod rasped, his voice barely audible.

A servant hurried out, returning moments later with Nicolas of Damascus. The advisor's face was a mask of calm, though his eyes betrayed the weight of what he knew was coming. He knelt by Herod's bedside, his hands folded neatly.

"My king," Nicolas said softly. "What do you require?"

Herod's lips twisted into something resembling a smile, though it was more grimace than expression. "You've always been at my side, Nicolas. Even now, you stay while others wait for me to die. Loyal to the end."

"I have served you faithfully," Nicolas replied, his tone measured. "It is my duty."

Herod's hand, skeletal and trembling, reached for Nicolas but stopped short. "Duty. Yes. Tell me, do you think they'll remember me as I was? Or will they only see the tyrant, the butcher?"

Nicolas hesitated, then answered carefully. "History will see both, my king. A man of great ambition and vision, but also a man who bore the weight of his choices."

Herod chuckled, a dry, rattling sound. "Weight of choices. That's a poetic way to say I destroyed everything I touched."

His thoughts drifted, slipping between the present and the past. He saw the walls of Masada rising against the desert sky, the gleaming marble of Caesarea Maritima's harbor, the restored Temple in Jerusalem standing as a beacon of his reign. He had built monuments to eternity, but the faces of those he had lost haunted him just as vividly.

Mariamne appeared in his mind's eye; her beauty unmarred by the bitterness of her death. She looked at him with the same mix of love and sorrow she had carried in life.

"Did you ever forgive me?" Herod murmured; his words slurred by weakness.

Nicolas frowned. "My king?"

Herod's eyes glazed over, unfocused. "Mariamne. She's here. Always here. I see her when I close my eyes. I hear her voice in the silence."

The room felt colder as night fell, the flickering lamplight casting shadows that danced across the walls. Herod's breathing grew labored, each exhale rattling in his chest. A physician entered, flanked by attendants carrying vials of ointments and elixirs.

They worked in silence, their hands steady but their faces grim.

"Will it stop the pain?" Herod asked, his voice a whisper.

The physician bowed his head. "It will ease your suffering, my king."

Herod's lips curled into a sneer. "Ease my suffering? You cannot undo a lifetime in a single vial."

As the hours dragged on, Herod's mind wandered further into the labyrinth of his memories. He saw his mother, Cypros, warning him of betrayal in her stern, unyielding voice. He saw his sons, Alexander and Aristobulus, their faces filled with the defiance that had sealed their fate. And then Antipater, his eldest, whose ambition had mirrored his own, leading to their mutual destruction.

"A family of ruins," Herod muttered. "I built a kingdom and tore down my bloodline."

Nicolas leaned closer; his brow furrowed. "My king, your legacy is more than that. You built cities, restored the Temple. You united a fractured land."

Herod's eyes locked onto Nicolas with startling clarity. "And for what? To leave it to sons who will tear it apart. To Rome, who will carve it into pieces? Tell me, Nicolas, was it worth it?"

Nicolas's silence was answer enough.

The end came slowly, creeping inevitability that filled the room with an unbearable tension. Herod's attendants returned, their faces pale as they hovered at the edges of the chamber. A priest stood near the doorway, murmuring prayers, though his voice wavered.

Herod's breaths grew shallower, his chest rising and falling with agonizing slowness. The pain that had defined his final days seemed to fade, replaced by a strange calm. He turned his head toward the window, where the first light of dawn painted the sky in soft hues of orange and pink.

"The sun rises," Herod murmured. "Even now, it rises."

Nicolas leaned in, his voice steady. "It is a new day, my king."

Herod's lips twitched, as if forming a final thought, a final word. But no sound came. His body stilled; his gaze fixed on the horizon. The king of Judea was no more.

The silence that followed was profound, as if the world itself held its breath. Nicolas rose slowly, his hands trembling as he closed Herod's eyes. The attendants bowed their heads, their fear replaced by a tentative reverence.

Outside the palace, the city began to stir. Merchants prepared their stalls, children ran through the streets, and the hum of life carried on, indifferent to the passing of a king. Herod's death would ripple through Judea and beyond, but for now, the world remained unchanged.

Nicolas stood by the window, watching the sunrise with a heavy heart. Herod had been a man of contradictions, a ruler of great achievements and devastating flaws. His legacy would be debated for centuries, but at this moment, all that remained was the stillness of a life ended and the quiet promise of a new day.

EPILOGUE: LEGACY

The sun hung low in the Judean sky, its golden light casting long shadows over the land Herod had ruled. The Temple in Jerusalem, his crowning achievement, gleamed atop the hill, its white stone walls radiant against the heavens. Pilgrims gathered in its courtyards, their prayers rising like a murmured symphony, while merchants hawked their wares in the bustling streets below. To the casual observer, the Temple was a marvel, a beacon of faith and architectural brilliance. But to those who knew its story, it was also a monument to Herod's ambition—and the suffering it had wrought.

Yoram, now an old man, leaned on his staff as he stood near the Temple's outer gates. His hands, gnarled and calloused from years of labor, rested on the polished wood. He had been one of the many who had toiled to bring Herod's vision to life, his sweat and blood etched into the very stones that now inspired awe. The years had not dulled his memories, nor had they softened his reflections on the man who had commissioned such grandeur.

"He built it for God," a young man beside him said, gazing up at the towering structure with wide eyes.

Yoram shook his head, a bitter smile tugging at his lips. "He built it for himself. Don't let the gold and marble fool you. Herod was no servant of God. He served only his own glory."

The young man frowned. "But look at what he left behind. Surely a man who built something so magnificent cannot be entirely wicked."

Yoram's gaze lingered on the Temple, his mind awash with memories. He thought of the laborers who had died during its construction, their bodies broken by the king's relentless demands. He thought of Herod's paranoia, the blood that had soaked the palace floors, the cries of innocents silenced by his decrees.

"Greatness always comes at a cost," Yoram said finally. "But sometimes the cost is too high. Remember that."

Far from Jerusalem, in the heart of Rome, Quintus Varro stood in the grand halls of Augustus' palace. The envoy had returned from Judea bearing news of Herod's death and the state of his divided kingdom. He presented his report with the precision of a man who understood the stakes of his words.

"Herod is gone," Varro began, his voice steady. "His kingdom, as expected, is already fracturing. His sons vie for power, each seeking to assert dominance over their inheritance. Judea remains volatile, its people weary from decades of oppression and excess."

Augustus, seated in his ornate chair, listened with an inscrutable expression. His advisors flanked him, their eyes flickering with interest as Varro continued.

"Herod was a man of immense ambition," Varro said, "but also of deep insecurity. He built monuments to his power, yet those same monuments stand as reminders of the suffering he inflicted. His paranoia destroyed his family, his alliances, and ultimately his peace of mind. He is a cautionary tale, Caesar, of what happens when ambition outweighs reason."

Augustus's gaze drifted toward a map of the empire, his fingers tracing the edges of Judea. "And what of his legacy? Will the people remember him as a king or a tyrant?"

Varro hesitated. "Both, Caesar. He was a man of contradictions. To some, he was a builder of greatness, to others, a destroyer of lives. His name will endure, but so too will the scars he left behind."

In the years that followed Herod's death, his kingdom fractured under the weight of its divisions. Archelaus ruled Judea and Samaria, but his heavy-handed governance stoked rebellion and unrest. Antipas governed Galilee and Perea, his ambitions tempered by Roman oversight. Philip, the quietest of the brothers, maintained a tenuous peace in the territories east of the Jordan. The unity Herod had fought to maintain was gone, replaced by a fragile balance that teetered on the edge of collapse.

The Temple, however, remained. Pilgrims continued to flock to its gates, their awe undiminished by the shadow of its creator. For many, it was a symbol of faith, a connection to something greater than themselves. But for others, like Yoram, it was a reminder of the price paid for one man's vision.

One evening, as the sun dipped below the horizon, casting the city in hues of amber and crimson, Yoram sat with his grandchildren near the city's walls. The children, full of curiosity, asked about the Temple and the king who had built it.

"Was Herod a great king?" one of them asked, her eyes wide.

Yoram sighed, his gaze drifting toward the distant silhouette of the Temple. "He was a man who wanted to be remembered," he said. "And he will be. But greatness is not just about what you build. It is about what you leave behind in the hearts of others. Herod built walls and palaces, but he tore down trust and love. In the end, only you can decide if that is greatness."

The children were silent, their young minds grappling with the complexity of his words. Yoram placed a hand on the nearest child's shoulder, his grip firm but gentle.

"Remember this," he said. "The stones may stand, but it is the people who carry the true weight of a king's reign."

In Rome, Augustus decreed that Judea would remain under the supervision of the empire, its governance carefully monitored to prevent further instability. Herod's name was spoken in the Senate as both a warning and a marvel, a ruler whose ambition had reached the heavens but whose paranoia had dragged him to the depths. His life became the subject of stories, his deeds recounted with a mix of admiration and horror.

Back in Judea, the Temple continued to dominate the skyline, its grandeur undiminished. But as the years passed, the people began to speak less of Herod and more of the lives they lived in its shadow. The markets bustled, the streets filled with the laughter of children, and the city pulsed with life. The king who had once commanded their every thought became a figure of the past; his legacy absorbed into the fabric of history.

And so, Herod's story came to an end, his reign a tapestry of contradictions. He had built cities, fortified kingdoms, and restored a sacred Temple, leaving a mark that would endure for centuries. But he had also sown fear, mistrust, and grief, his paranoia consuming everything he had sought to protect.

The Temple stood as a silent witness, its walls bearing the weight of both glory and sorrow. And in the quiet corners of Judea, where the common people gathered, Herod's name was spoken in hushed tones, a reminder that even the greatest rulers are but men, their legacies shaped as much by their failures as by their triumphs.

AFTERWORD

Herod the Great remains one of history's most enigmatic figures—a ruler whose name evokes both awe and revulsion. Through the centuries, scholars, historians, and storytellers have grappled with the contradictions of his reign. Was he a visionary who sought to secure the future of Judea, or a tyrant consumed by ambition and paranoia? The answer, as with so many figures of antiquity, lies somewhere in between.

Herod's architectural achievements were unparalleled. The Second Temple, Masada, Caesarea Maritima, and other monumental projects stand as testaments to his ambition and genius. These structures were not just edifices of stone and marble; they were symbols of his enduring desire to carve his name into the annals of history. Yet, beneath their grandeur lies the untold suffering of countless laborers, the human cost of a legacy forged in blood and sweat.

Beyond his buildings, Herod's life was marked by the complexities of power. He navigated the treacherous waters of Roman politics with cunning and resolve, securing his throne through alliances, betrayals, and sheer force of will. His relationships, however, were another matter. The deaths of his wife Mariamne, his sons, and numerous others paint a portrait of a man plagued by insecurity, whose paranoia eroded the very bonds that should have sustained him.

This novel has sought to capture the essence of Herod's life, blending historical fact with creative interpretation to illuminate both the man and the myth. While history provides the scaffolding, fiction fills in the emotional and psychological spaces, offering a glimpse into the thoughts and motivations of a ruler who defied the limits of his time. It is not meant to judge Herod, but to understand him—to explore the forces that shaped him and the choices that defined him.

As you close this book, consider the duality of Herod's legacy. He was a builder and a destroyer, a king and a tyrant, a man whose achievements and failures remain inextricably linked. His story is a reminder of the enduring complexity of power, the price of ambition, and the fragile line between greatness and infamy.

Thank you for journeying through the life of Herod the Great. May his story spark reflection on the nature of leadership, the weight of legacy, and the human cost of ambition.

ACKNOWLEDGEMENT

Writing *Herod: The Architect of Power* has been a journey of discovery, reflection, and collaboration. This book would not have been possible without the support and contributions of many remarkable individuals.

To my wife, Subhashini, your unwavering encouragement, wisdom, and belief in my vision have been the foundation upon which this work was built. You are my greatest ally and my constant source of inspiration. Thank you for standing by me through every challenge and triumph.

To my daughter, Sasha, whose boundless curiosity and joy remind me of the importance of storytelling. Your laughter and love have been a beacon of light throughout this process.

To my friends and family, who provided invaluable feedback and motivation, thank you for your insights and for believing in this story as much as I did.

A heartfelt thanks to the historians, scholars, and writers whose works have illuminated the complexities of Herod's life and times. Your research and dedication to understanding history provided the scaffolding for this fictional exploration.

To my readers, thank you for embarking on this journey into the world of ancient Judea. Your passion for history and literature fuels my drive to tell these stories. If you enjoyed this book, I kindly ask you to leave a review on Amazon. Your feedback not only helps other readers discover the story but also supports my work as an author.

Finally, to all those who have ever grappled with the complexities of power, legacy, and ambition—this book is for you. May it spark thought, debate, and a deeper understanding of the forces that shape us and the histories we create.

ABOUT THE AUTHOR

D. Deckker

Dinesh Deckker is a best selling author and a seasoned expert in digital marketing, boasting more than 20 years of experience in the industry. His strong academic foundation includes a BA in Business Management from Wrexham University (UK), a Bachelor of Computer Science from IIC University (Cambodia), an MBA from the University of Gloucestershire (UK), and ongoing PhD studies in Marketing.

Deckker's career is as versatile as his academic pursuits. He is also a prolific author, having written over 100+ books across various subjects.

He has further honed his writing skills through a variety of specialized courses. His qualifications include:

Children Acquiring Literacy Naturally from UC Santa Cruz, USA
Creative Writing Specialization from Wesleyan University, USA
Writing for Young Readers Commonwealth Education Trust
Introduction to Early Childhood from The State University of New York
Introduction to Psychology from Yale University
Academic English: Writing Specialization University of California,

Irvine,
Writing and Editing Specialization from University of Michigan
Writing and Editing: Word Choice University of Michigan
Sharpened Visions: A Poetry Workshop from CalArts, USA
Grammar and Punctuation from University of California, Irvine, USA
Teaching Writing Specialization from Johns Hopkins University
Advanced Writing from University of California, Irvine, USA
English for Journalism from University of Pennsylvania, USA
Creative Writing: The Craft of Character from Wesleyan University, USA
Creative Writing: The Craft of Setting from Wesleyan University
Creative Writing: The Craft of Plot from Wesleyan University, USA
Creative Writing: The Craft of Style from Wesleyan University, USA

Dinesh's diverse educational background and commitment to lifelong learning have equipped him with a deep understanding of various writing styles and educational techniques. His works often reflect his passion for storytelling, education, and technology, making him a versatile and engaging author.

BOOKS BY THIS AUTHOR

Kashyapa: Chronicles Of Sigiriya : Historical Fiction Novel

Step into the shadowed halls of 5th-century Sri Lanka, where ambition, betrayal, and destiny collide beneath the majestic rock fortress of Sigiriya.

In a land of intrigue and superstition, King Kashyapa seeks to immortalize his legacy by constructing a breathtaking citadel atop a towering rock. But as the walls rise, so too do whispers of treachery and curses. Haunted by the ghost of his father, the defiance of his court, and his own unraveling mind, Kashyapa must navigate a web of political intrigue, forbidden rituals, and the weight of his guilt.

Condemned By Law: A Story Of Betrayal, Judgment, And Sacrifice

"A forbidden love. An unforgiving law. A story of courage and tragedy that will stay with you long after the final page."

In 1533, the Buggery Act cast a dark shadow over England, condemning love that dared to defy societal norms. Spanning centuries, Condemned by Law tells the intertwined stories of Thomas Hale, a lawyer torn between ambition and conscience as he witnesses the Act's creation, and John Preston and Samuel Carter, two men in 1835 whose forbidden bond leads them to the gallows.

The Complete Guide To Greek Mythology: Gods, Heroes, And The Mysteries Of Olympus

Unveil the fascinating world of Greek mythology with The Complete Guide to Greek Mythology: Gods, Heroes, and the Mysteries of Olympus. This comprehensive guide explores the timeless myths that have shaped Western culture for millennia.

Delve into the lives of the powerful gods of Mount Olympus, from Zeus, the ruler of the skies, to Athena, goddess of wisdom and war. Learn about the heroic quests of figures like Heracles, Perseus, and Theseus, whose feats continue to captivate readers of all ages. Explore the depths of the underworld with Hades and encounter mythical creatures like the Minotaur, Medusa, and Pegasus.

The Light Of Bethlehem: A Story Of Hope And Light - Nativity Story Novel

Step into the timeless story of Bethlehem with this deeply human retelling of the Nativity. The Light of Bethlehem invites readers to witness the miracle through the eyes of those who were there —Mary, Joseph, the shepherds, and the wise men. This novel beautifully captures their courage, love, and sacrifice, weaving a rich tapestry of hope and resilience.

Made in the USA
Columbia, SC
22 January 2025